THE BOY WITH THE TIGER'S HEART

THE BOY WITH THE TIGER'S HEART

LINDA COGGIN

HOT
KEY
BOOKS

First published in Great Britain in 2014 by Hot Key Books
Northburgh House, 10 Northburgh Street, London EC1V 0AT

Copyright © Linda Coggin 2014
Cover illustration copyright © Levente Szabo 2014

The moral rights of the author have been asserted.

A CIP catalogue record for this book is available from the British Library.

ISBN: 978-1-4714-0458-0
1

This book is typeset in 11.75pt Sabon using Atomik ePublisher

Printed and bound by Clays Ltd, St Ives Plc

www.hotkeybooks.com

Hot Key Books is part of the Bonnier Publishing Group
www.bonnierpublishing.com

for Phoebe

When all the dangerous cliffs are fenced off, all the trees that might fall on people are cut down, all of the insects that bite have been poisoned – and all of the grizzlies are dead because they are occasionally dangerous, the wilderness will not be made safe. Rather, the safety will have destroyed the wilderness.

R. Yorke Edwards
Former Director, Royal British Columbia Museum,
Canadian Environmentalist

Chapter 1

The snow falls heavily that night and in the morning lies in deep drifts, which smooth over the shapes of the jagged rocks and grassy knolls. It hides the bog holes that lie at the edge of the marshes and covers the wrecks of the burnt-out cars. It sparkles like crushed diamonds. It is pure, white and perfect, but to the girl when she looks out from her hiding place it is a bad omen.

Today the trackers will surely find them.

She pulls her fur-lined hood over her face and scans the horizon.

The sun is low in the sky, a fiery ball that tips

the distant hills with a stroke of pink. Nothing moves, but already there are some tiny, rare prints in the snow – hare, weasel, the random hopping marks of the carrion crow.

Some loose snow collapses on her from the canopy of scrub under which they'd made their nest. The only sound in the muffled silence. She licks the cool ice that falls onto her lips.

The bear has gone.

It must have left some time in the night. Although she can see the tracks leading back into the forest, they are now only blurred outlines where the snow has continued to fall on them.

She collects her things and stands up, her limbs stiff with the cold. The ground on which she'd lain down is still brown, like a pool of bracken in the white landscape.

She follows the prints.

Chapter 2

Two days earlier.

From the back of his pen, the bear watches the police officer touch his cap and lean against the barn door, his hands in his jacket pockets.

'We need to see that permit, Tom.'

'Since when?' replies Thomas Bailey, the bear's keeper.

'We've had complaints.'

'Complaints? What sort of complaints?' says Thomas Bailey, forking hay into the big cat's enclosure without looking round.

'That bear escaped again last week, didn't it?

The Nolans over at Meadow Sweet said it had gone through their rubbish.' The officer strolls over and looks around the barn.

'Didn't do any harm. He soon came back.'

'Look, folk round here have got it in for you.'

'So?'

'They think you're odd, a bit of a loner, keeping wild animals and that girl of yours – what's her name? Did you even give her one?'

'You keep her out of this.' Thomas walks towards him.

The officer shakes his head, beads of sweat gathering on his brow.

'We'll be back with a warrant. Please put that pitchfork down, Mr Bailey.'

'Get off my land. You're trespassing.'

'You'd best tell that girl to get her things packed,' the officer says, backing off. 'She can't go on living here with you. We all know where she came from.'

'I said – keep her out of this.'

'It's just not right a girl like that should have no proper schooling.'

'You're trespassing on my property.' Thomas jabs at the air with his pitchfork. 'Get off my land or I'll set one of the big cats on you.'

'Don't threaten me, Mr Bailey. That girl should be educated properly. She should be in Dissville. You can't just keep her as an experiment.'

The officer reaches the door, his hand shaking as he moves the catch.

'I'm going to have to report you, you know.'

'Leave us alone! And don't bother to come back with no permit.' He tightens his lips. 'You'll be sorry for your visit today. Just you see.'

At dusk, Thomas Bailey goes round his farm unlocking all the gates and doors. The bear is the last to be set free and the only one to see the keeper put his gun to his head and pull the trigger.

It is the Nolans at Meadow Sweet who report the escaped animals.

When they hear something going through their dustbins again Mr Nolan comes out with a stick, expecting to see the bear. What he sees in the dying evening light is a huge leopard with the chicken carcass from their Sunday lunch in its jaws.

The police station's switchboard is jamming with calls.

'There's a zebra in my garden!'

'There's a lion prowling about and our cat's gone missing.'

'There's a tiger frightening our horses.'

Within half an hour there will be a fleet of police cars and vans surrounding Thomas Bailey's property and a helicopter circling overhead.

With the sound of the gun going off, a girl appears from behind some straw bales.

The bear eyes her, creeping slowly out on all fours. He likes her. When she sees the bear is alone she stands up.

She is tall and thin with long hair the colour of winter wheat, which falls down to her waist. Her eyes are the shape of almonds and the green of faded moss and she is kind to him.

She isn't like others.

'What's happened?' she says to him in a low voice.

The bear, who Thomas Bailey named Abel Dancer, puts his head up and she ruffles his ears. Then she strokes his chest, which carries the shape of a crescent moon in his fur, and he makes a soft, grunting sound that makes her smile.

'Wah,' he says. 'Wah.'

He stands up on his hind legs and walks out of his open cage and goes over to the body of her guardian, hidden by some grain bins.

She looks down at Thomas Bailey, and is struck by how the mess of him is much like that of any other dead animal whose insides were on the outside. She doesn't want to think about how he died – just that he had.

Her mind is working fast though. She knows she has to get out, and as quickly as possible. Thomas had told her she would be put into care in Dissville if they found her. Worse, probably, she would become an object of curiosity – observed, studied and questioned. What was it like to be brought up by wild dogs? Do you feel human?

Who were your parents?

How could she answer any of these questions?

She had been a small child.

She covers Thomas up with straw, debating whether or not to take his gun. She picks it up and turns it round in her hand, then she looks down at her small pack and decides against it. She has her crossbow and knife and that is all she needs.

The bear follows her willingly across the fields towards the woods. Sometimes he runs on all fours but mostly he moves on his back legs, creating a huge, monstrous shape in the fading light. He trusts her.

They will need each other.

As they near the woods the girl looks back. The escaped animals have triggered off the security lights, which shine past the buildings and high fences and fan across the fields.

The wood becomes dense very quickly with a thick canopy overhead. A huge fir faces out towards Thomas Bailey's farm.

'You're going to have to let me climb on your back,' she says, stopping underneath the tree and looking up. 'I just need to get hold of that first branch.'

Once up in the tree she calls to the bear. Since his escape to the Nolans' property he has discovered that climbing trees is one of the things he loves doing most and, putting his forelegs around the trunk, he pulls himself up into the branches.

The faint sound of police sirens can be heard coming up the long track, along with the *chop chop* sound of a helicopter. The girl shrinks back into the tree and watches the cars pull up outside the building.

A lion still prowls inside the fence and the girl can see a pair of wolves run towards the woods when the trucks pull up. As the guns go off she jumps. One of the wolves falls immediately; the other manages to get a little further before it too is shot.

There is another volley of gunshot and now the lion lies dead and the night air is filled with the sound of rifle fire.

The girl pushes her face into the bear's chest to block out the sound. Her eyes sting and when she lifts her head she feels cold tears roll down her cheeks. This is the first time she can ever remember crying and she is surprised at how salty tears taste.

They stay in the tree all night and, as the first light of morning rises in the sky, she looks across to the farm and sees the trucks and cars have gone. It seems quiet.

'Stay here, Bear,' she whispers, squeezing past him to climb down the tree. 'Whatever happens, stay here till I get back. And if I don't get back, run for it!'

Abel Dancer tries to follow her down the tree but she lifts her finger and says, 'No!' He watches her jump down from the bottom branch and creep out into the field.

'Wah. Wah,' he says.

She moves slowly, on all fours. The early morning dew soaks through her clothing but the long grass protects her from any searching eyes. The bodies of the wolves have been moved but when she approaches the building the stench of death reaches her nose. There, laid out like trophies along the track, are the rest of the bodies.

Six Bengal tigers.

Eight mountain lions.

A panther.

A cheetah.

Three monkeys.

Four more wolves.

One leopard.

Probably they had been the only ones of their kind left. Every animal considered wild by the Authorities had been killed, for fear of the animals turning on them as their habitat disappeared. This was one of the new laws of Dissville.

She feels the stinging in her eyes again but this time no tears fall.

'There's still a bear and a leopard loose, and we're not too sure how many wolves there were.'

Voices are approaching her from the side of the barn.

She runs and hides behind one of Thomas Bailey's old trucks, ducking down just as the figures of two men come round the corner.

'We'll find them today, I expect.'

The men stop by the dead animals, one of them touching the body of the lion with his boot.

'Like going on safari, wasn't it?'

She hears them chuckle and a streak of fury rises in her body. She could take them out, both of them, like they had the animals. Her hand goes to her side. Her knife is there, belted round her waist, but she'd need the crossbow and she has left it in her bag, up in the tree with the bear.

'The tracker dogs are coming and they've got some expert in. Also there's that thermal-imaging thing in the helicopter. That's bound to pick 'em out. It's top priority. Bolverk's orders. Imagine what damage a hungry leopard and a bear could do,' one of the men says.

'With any luck they'll eat each other!' laughs the other voice.

'Yeah – that would be neat! Rumour has it that guy did it in revenge. Apparently he liked the idea of his animals terrorising his interfering neighbours.'

'Really? Do you know how he died?'

'They reckon that weird girl of his did it. Her fingerprints were all over the gun. Quite a thank-you after all he did for her.'

The man grunts. 'Mind you, *he* was weird too. Gave all his animals names but never gave her one.'

The girl catches her breath. For a moment she feels the urge to show herself and tell them she had found him dead, that she would never do anything to harm him, that she had grown to love him. She remembers how he taught her with great patience, praising her when she did well. But she stops herself as she remembers his warning and shrinks back into the side of the truck.

'They say he went off the rails after his wife and son died in that fire,' the voice continues.

'Oh, yeah – I think I heard about that. The boy was only a nipper, wasn't he?'

There is silence for a while as they wander along the line of carcasses then, in the distance, the girl hears the low rumble of a truck coming up the drive. When the men move round the corner of the barn to meet the vehicle she springs up and races back across the field.

She runs fast and straight, her head down, her hands clenched, all the time thinking about what the man had said. She had lived with Thomas Bailey for seven years and in all that time had no idea that he had had a wife and a son. He had been a private man and she seldom met anyone else. Her knowledge of the human race was very limited.

She throws herself down into the long grass just as the posse of bounty hunters turn the corner. She lies still for a while, then covers the rest of the distance on her stomach.

When she gets back to the fir tree the bear has gone. Her bag is on the ground underneath, still attached to one of the broken branches that lie scattered on the forest floor.

Chapter 3

When Abel Dancer tries to move onto another branch he falls, crashing through the canopy and landing in a heap at the bottom of the tree. He can knock back a fizzy drink from a bottle and dance a jig but there are some basic things he still has to deal with.

He is hungry now and goes in search of something to eat.

He is so busy tucking into his newfound feast of berries that he doesn't hear the girl approach him.

'You're a bad bear!' she says. 'I told you to stay where you were. We have to stick together.'

The bear lowers his head.

'Wah. Wah,' he says.

'You don't remember, do you? In fact you've probably no idea what I'm talking about.'

She plucks a handful of berries off the bush and crams them into her mouth.

'We have to move on. They're going to hunt us down. Bolverk's orders – whoever he is. We must cross the river to wash away our scent.'

Abel Dancer might not have heard the girl creep up on him but he hears the first sound of the tracker dogs as they are let out of the back of the van. She hears them too.

'Hurry!' she says, breaking into a run. 'We've got to get to that river.'

The bear finds it difficult keeping up with her, alternating between running on all fours and moving on his back legs, which is slowing her down.

A wind has blown up which muffles the sound of the tracker dogs but there is a distinct *chop chop* sound coming up over the brow of the hill. The weather is looking threatening with the gathering of heavy black storm clouds.

The girl pulls the bear towards a large bush and crouches down. She peers into the sky through the branches. The helicopter is on the horizon, a thin red beam moving from it across the landscape. It is getting nearer and nearer, the noise from its blades so loud now she has to cover her head.

Chop! Chop!

Beside her, the bear is becoming agitated. He is moaning and making a blowing noise between his teeth, tossing his head from side to side, trying to escape from the piercing sound in his ears. She hangs onto him, making soothing noises in her throat and pulling him closer to her.

Chop! Chop!

The wind from the blades is so strong now that it tears the leaves from the undergrowth and blows dust and debris into the air. The red light from the chopper is dancing only a few metres away from them, when there is a crack of lightning. The helicopter lurches forward and seems to rock, dipping and diving until finally it turns away and flies back towards the brow of the hill, its engine coughing and spluttering.

She grabs the bear and pulls him onto his feet.

Thinking she is wrestling with him he places his arms on her shoulders and pushes against her, knocking her to the ground. She remembers, as she rolls out of the way, that Thomas Bailey had rescued him from a bear wrestler, who had muzzled him and dragged him round from town to town, rewarding him with bottles of Coca-Cola.

Abel Dancer stops and turns his head. He can hear them again – distant choking, panting sounds of three or four dogs straining at their leashes, pulling their handlers as they pick up his scent.

He drops down on all fours and nudges the girl with his nose.

'What's up, Bear?'

She stands up and looks into the distance. 'You can hear them – can't you? We've got to move. Get to that river.'

There is a roll of thunder that echoes round the rocks and the forest, then another crash of lightning. She looks at the bear. For a moment he is lit up – a large dark figure against the white flash of light, his eyes staring at her. She wonders if he is frightened. She too can hear the dogs now and something inside her tightens around her chest like a snake. She feels her heart quicken.

'Run!' she shouts. 'Run!'

Perhaps it is the sound of the dogs, or the smell of fear he picks up from the girl, but something helps the bear to find his speed. No longer caged, he finds he is fast – his four legs working better and quicker than moving, human-like, on his hind legs.

They run towards the brow of the hill, the wind slashing frozen rain into their faces. When they reach the top the girl looks back. Behind them are the men and their dogs but in front of them, down the other side, sweeps the river.

They run and fall and tumble towards the water, slipping on the loose stones and tufts of grass, a voice in the girl's head urging her on and on.

'Don't look back,' it says. 'Don't look back.'

They reach the banks of the river and carry on running into the freezing water. When it reaches her waist the girl frees her feet from the riverbed and kicks out, swimming like a dog, her head high, one arm paddling out in front of her, the other holding her pack above the surface. She turns her head to look back at the bear. He is floating in the water, a look of pleasure on his face.

'No!' she shouts. 'You've got to *swim*. I know you can swim. All bears can swim.' He rolls over on his front, lolling his head from side to side.

'*And dogs can swim too!*' she pants. 'So get a move on!'

By the time she reaches the other side, the girl is gasping with the cold. She pulls herself out and, panting, stumbles towards a group of shrubs. The dogs are hot on their trail but still they have not reached the brow of the hill. The bear is now sniffing around the shoreline.

'Hurry – before they see you,' she calls out. 'Hide! They're coming.'

But the bear takes his time, stopping to check out some new smell here, some possible thing to eat there.

'Oh, hurry! Come quick!' she calls again. 'Why are you being so slow? They'll shoot you and then you'll never be able to sniff anything again.'

The bear reaches the shrubs just as a large dog appears on top of the hill. The dog stops and looks around, then lifts its muzzle and sniffs the air. The girl shrinks back into the bushes and watches as two other dogs join it, growling loudly.

'They're onto something,' she hears a voice shout out. 'I hope they get them before they cross that damn river.'

The dogs are whining now and running down towards the shoreline, their tails wagging and their noses skimming the surface of the ground.

Four men stand silhouetted against the dark sky, guns slung over their shoulders.

When the dogs reach the water's edge they stop and bark.

'Damn. They've already crossed. We've lost their scent. How the hell are we going to cross that river now?' one of the men says, lowering his gun to his side.

'Perhaps they'll freeze to death,' answers another voice. 'It's a mighty wide stretch of water.'

'Yeah. Looks like we're in for a snowstorm too.'

Their voices carry across the water and the girl

can hear everything they say.

'So what do you know about her?' one of them asks.

'I heard he rescued her from a pack of dogs when she was a kid. Wild, she was.'

'Did you ever see her?' the third man asks.

'Only once, shortly after he got her. She growled and spat at me – it was kinda scary. She was a pretty little thing until she did that.' He pauses. 'We won't tell Bolverk. We'll leave it for tonight and cross over to the other side in the morning. With any luck we'll pick up their tracks tomorrow. They won't get far.' But he picks up his gun and releases the catch.

'What yer doin'?' The fourth man moves forward, holding his gun up in front of him.

'See them there bushes? I wouldn't be surprised if they weren't hiding in there. Couldn't have got much further. Let's just take a pop shot to check it out.'

The girl sees the men take aim and grabs hold of the bear's neck, pushing her rucksack in front to protect them.

'Get down!' she whispers. 'Whatever happens, please don't move.'

They hear the first shot and the sound of splitting stone as the bullet falls short of the shrubs. The bear attempts to struggle free as she tries to calm him.

'It's OK. It's OK. Keep still now.'

The second gun goes off and the shot hits the bushes a few metres to the right of them. Abel Dancer roars and pulls away from her.

'No!' she shouts. 'Don't! They'll kill you!'

But he is up and tears out of the back of the shrubs, bounding up the other side towards open ground.

'There it goes! What did I tell you?' shouts one of the men. 'Get the bastard.'

A volley of shots crack across the rocks, pinging off the stones and the earth as the bear runs away from the river and the girl.

She can't look; instead she puts her hands over her ears and waits for it all to stop.

The guns carry on for two or three minutes. Then she hears one of the men whistle to his dog.

'Let's go. That snowstorm is on its way. We'll look for the body tomorrow.'

When she thinks they have gone, she wriggles out of her hiding place, grabs her things and looks across the river, just to be sure.

'*The damn river*,' she says to herself. 'The *damn* river. Why call it that? Without that there'd be no water. How ignorant people are.' She shakes her head and turns away. Behind her there is marshland and woodland in the distance, but not much shelter until then. The freezing rain has turned to snow, which whips across the marshes and makes running hard. She battles her way through it towards the trees, all the time calling in a low voice for the bear. As she runs, her eyes dart over the landscape, looking for him. Sometimes she is deceived by a shape in the distance that only turns out to be a boulder or a mound of grass.

She reaches the wood and skirts around it, looking for a suitable place to curl up and sleep. She finds some brambles and bracken and, turning round and round with her body, makes herself a bed.

It is dark by now, and the snow has stopped. A clear midnight-blue sky hangs over her, lit by a thousand or more stars. She looks up at the constellation. There is Ursa Major – the Great Bear – twinkling above her head as if the bear himself is keeping watch over her.

She is a light sleeper and has only dozed off for a moment, when she hears a rustling sound nearby. She reaches out for her knife and slowly turns onto all fours. Not far away she can hear heavy breathing. She holds her own breath and waits for her eyes to grow accustomed to the dark. Something is moving towards her.

She crouches back into the bushes and watches as a dark shape creeps into the shrubs.

'Bear!' she cries out.

Her hand moves away from her knife and she leans forward as Abel Dancer's face comes through the bush, sniffing her body with his wet nose. She hugs him.

'Wah,' he says.

'I thought they'd got you. You were lucky, but you can't run faster than a bullet.' She tries to stop smiling at him. How will he take her seriously if she's got a big grin on her face? 'Next time keep your ground.'

They curl up together and sleep and when she wakes in the morning the snow has come and the bear has gone.

She follows the prints.

Chapter 4

Abel Dancer trots off into the forest, occasionally stopping by some bushes, where he helps himself to berries, their purple juice staining his prints in the snow. They are easy to follow, and this bothers her. A child could follow their route.

She stops. A second set of prints enters from dense shrubs to the right and follows those of the bear. The hairs on the back of her neck begin to bristle. The prints belong to a large cat. The missing leopard. And she knows it will be hungry.

She guesses by the size of the prints that it was the female that was shot. The male – known as

John Hunter – was more aggressive and Thomas Bailey had never let her go near him.

'These leopards are not pets you can play with like that bear, especially the male one,' he'd said. 'He will not see you as a friend but as something to eat. If you put your hand up to defend yourself he'll have your arm. Then he will have the rest of you. Do not go near him.'

In spite of Abel Dancer's size and claws she doesn't think he'll stand much chance in a fight.

She takes her bow out of her bag, slips an arrow into place and then begins to run, soundlessly in the eerie silence, her weight hardly making an impression on the already deep and frozen snow.

The forest becomes denser; the snow, hanging on to the canopy of trees, blots out the light, and the path twists and turns deeper into the darkness. It is rare to find any trees left standing. Dissville cut down most of the woodlands, as they were considered dark and evil, a place where animals could hide and attack, a place where danger itself could hide.

But here, Thomas Bailey had protected this

small piece of woodland and had told her that without trees nothing can speak.

As she walks, she begins to dread turning a corner for fear of what will be there. At any moment she expects to find the dead body of the bear.

A snapping, growling noise cuts through the stillness, then something crashes through the undergrowth towards her, snorting heavily. She draws back her bow just as a dark shape barrels into her, sending her flying onto the ground. It carries on the way she has come and she lies there, the wind knocked out of her, watching Abel Dancer running away. She hauls herself up and carries on, entering a clearing where the snow is a muddle of footprints. A snarling sound above her head draws her eyes upwards. In a huge makeshift net swings the angry, clawing leopard and to one side, his bow about to let off an arrow, stands a boy.

She stares at him.

'What do you think you're doing?'

The boy swings round, lowering his bow when

he sees the girl aiming at him, and says nothing.

She holds him in her sight, unwavering.

'If you kill that leopard I'll . . . I'll . . . kill *you*,' she says.

His eyes dart from the swinging leopard to the girl.

'What's it to you?'

'You shouldn't kill it.'

He shrugs his shoulders.

'Where are you from anyway?' he says.

The girl says nothing but continues to stare at him. He is shorter than her and well built. She notices a length of string holds up his trousers and he is wearing an old leather sleeveless jacket. His red hair is caked in mud and he has a scar that looks fresh down one side of his face.

'I've never seen you before,' he says.

'That's because I've never seen *you*.'

The girl looks back at the leopard, which is panting with exhaustion, and lowers her bow.

'Where did you get that scar? Did the cat give it you?'

When he goes to touch it with his hand she

reacts quickly, bringing the bow back and tightening her grip.

'My stepfather,' he says.

She doesn't ask any more, just nods.

'Will you let that cat go now?'

The boy grunts and moves towards her. 'Look. Don't you need to eat? Are you rich enough to turn down a reward like this?'

'A reward?' she says.

'For anyone who catches one of these animals.'

'The bear too?'

'Where have you been? Don't you know about the rewards? People want these animals caught.'

'Why?'

'They're a danger. They're wild.'

The girl frowns. 'I don't know what you're talking about.'

She turns back in the direction she came in.

'Where are you going?' he says.

'I'm going to look for the bear.'

He leaves the leopard and follows her back down the path, slipping in the icy prints.

'What's your name?'

Large drops of water fall from the overhead branches. As quickly as the snow has come it is thawing.

'Bear,' she calls softly. 'Where are you, Bear?'

'I said, what's your name?'

'I don't have a name.'

'You must have a name.'

'Case sixteen,' she says.

'That's not a name.'

'It's what he called me.'

'Who?'

'The man I lived with.'

Abel Dancer stands under a tree on his back legs, swaying with agitation, his big paws up in the air.

'Wah,' he says.

'It's OK,' she says. 'No one's going to harm you.'

She turns back and glares at the boy.

The bear drops back onto all fours and she touches his ears.

'Wah. Wah.'

'Why did he call you that?' the boy says.

'I was his sixteenth case history I suppose.'

The leopard starts to roar again and there is a loud splitting of wood, which makes the boy jump. Leaving the girl he runs back up the path, the girl watching him as he flounders in the melting slush.

She hears him shout.

'It's gone! Oh no, it's gone!'

She leaves the bear where he is and runs after the boy, finding him examining his net, which lies cut on the forest floor.

'Who did this?' she says.

He shakes his head.

'I'm glad,' she says.

'And they've destroyed my hide.'

They look over to his den, which is now a pile of crumpled sticks and torn canvas.

'There's some crazy boy about. I've never seen him. But sometimes I know he's there, watching me. My mum says he comes from The Edge.'

The girl is not interested in why they think he is crazy. Normal and crazy are not different ends of the spectrum to her. They weave through each other like creepers, showing themselves only when there is someone there to judge their behaviour. People had thought *she* was crazy because she'd been nurtured by dogs until she was five, but to her it was perfectly normal. Normal to curl up with each other when they were tired, to eat raw meat when they could get it, to be part of a pack and to run as fast as the breeze. She leaves the boy and turns to go back to the bear.

'Do *you* have a name?' she calls over her shoulder.

'Caius,' he says.

She nods. 'And the other person? Does he have a name?'

Caius shrugs. 'I don't know.'

The girl and the bear make their way back towards the shore of the river, where the snow has now melted. The sun is still low in the sky but its warm rays remove the final traces of their footprints. She wonders when the dogs will be back. Maybe this time with the Bolverk person.

She thinks about what the boy has said.

In fact, she did know what he was talking

about. When she'd been living with the dogs there had been the Big Cull, when every wild animal was killed, or caught to be trained for people's amusement. That's how Abel Dancer had survived. He had become a dancing bear.

When Thomas Bailey had told her that her dog parents had been killed in the Cull she hadn't been able to understand.

'Men are frightened of The Wild,' he'd said.

Thomas Bailey had been kind to her. He'd taught her how to read and write, to walk on two legs instead of moving on all fours, how to speak. He taught her how to use a crossbow, a knife and a gun, but there were things he could never have taught her which she already knew. How to blend into the landscape, how to slow down her pulse and her heartbeat so she was almost undetectable and how to rip a carcass to shreds with her teeth.

'You know between right and wrong now, don't you?' Thomas Bailey had said to her. 'Don't lie, don't cheat, don't steal, and don't kill another human.'

Chapter 5

The girl sits on the shoreline and watches the bear in the water, forgetting for a moment the men who are tracking her.

She sees him catch a fish and smiles. It's a large silver-grey salmon, which flounders and flaps on the rock when he brings it back to her. He leaves it there and returns to the river. She knows it's meant for her, a gift which she rips into with her teeth, swallowing the pink flesh until there is only the skeleton of it left. Once she's satisfied her hunger she is able to think more clearly. She decides to find Caius and ask him more about The Edge. She also reminds herself to be cautious. They are still being hunted and at any moment, if she lets her guard down, they could be captured. And there is one other thing to watch out for. The leopard.

She knows it is dangerous and that by now it will be hungry.

She calls to the bear and he ambles out of the water, swallowing a fish and shaking himself violently.

'No!' she shouts at him. 'Stop it, will you? I'm soaked. I haven't got any more clothes to change into, you know.'

He pushes his wet head under her arms and she falls, laughing, into the mud.

When they reach the clearing where she'd seen Caius he has gone, but he's attempted to rebuild his den and mend the net. It lies hidden under branches and dead leaves and she has to pull on Abel Dancer's ears to stop him walking into it. *It's a good trap*, she admits to herself as she dismantles it and hangs it on a tree.

As she turns around, she stiffens. The bear is

not moving either and she strains her ears for a sound. It is so silent – and that is the trouble. It is the silence of something or someone who does not want to be heard. She moves her head slowly. There it is. The tiny sound of a twig snapping. Her hand goes to her belt and brings out the knife. The bear gazes into the trees but he is not lifting his nose to sniff, which, if it had been the leopard or a man – the sinister-sounding Bolverk perhaps – he would have done.

She is suddenly aware of someone behind her and swings around, bringing the knife near to her face, ready to attack. A boy is standing in the shadows and she thinks this must be the crazy person that Caius spoke about, although she doesn't know what crazy looks like. This boy is taller and older than her, with jet-black hair and the most curious eyes. They shine, a greeny-yellow in the half-light of the day, and his face, which she thinks quite beautiful, holds the traces of several scars that run across his cheeks. As he steps out towards her she notices that her heartbeat has quickened.

'Was it you that let the leopard go?' she asks him.

The boy nods and looks her up and down.

'You come from The Edge, don't you? That boy Caius said so.'

A frown crosses the boy's face but he doesn't answer her.

'I want to know about it,' she says.

The bear decides then that he wants her attention and he ambles over to her side and pushes her with his head, knocking her onto her knees. The knife flies out of her hand and lands in the mushy snow. By the time she has retrieved it the boy has disappeared. She gets up and tries to follow him but although there is a flurry of prints where he stood she cannot tell in which direction he's gone.

'Hey!' she calls several times. 'Won't you come back?' But the boy neither answers her nor returns.

Most of the snow has melted but the ground still holds Caius's footprints and she follows them out of the wood and onto a stretch of moorland where a bleak wind blows across the short tufts of heather and grass. She takes a gamble on which direction Caius has gone – occasionally evidences of his journey reassuring her; a thread from his clothing, a broken twig. But there is no sign of the other boy or the leopard.

After a couple of hours she sees a wisp of smoke rising above some trees and the beginning of some kind of civilisation – rusty tractor parts, piles of broken bottles, beer and old petrol cans, rusted gin traps and a mountain of tins.

When he sees the pile of bottles the bear leaves her side and begins to pick through them, trying to drain their contents into his mouth. But they only have drops of muddy rainwater and rotting leaves in them and do not hold the promise on their labels. Coca-Cola.

The smoke is coming from a wooden, ramshackle hut, which seems to be held up with corrugated iron and sheets of plastic. The girl and the bear wait until it grows dark, their ears pricked for any sound.

They hear it at the same time. A breaking of

branches to the side of them and a panting of two or three dogs coming towards them from the trees. The dogs begin a low growling and the girl sinks back, her crossbow at the ready.

They have found them.

She reckons she can deal with the dogs but the men would be different. Whatever happens, she is not going to give up without a fight.

An ugly mutt of a dog bursts through the darkness of the trees, a pit-bull type with a misshapen head, slavering jaws and a big barrel chest. It starts to bark when it sees the bear and a second dog, a skinny brindled mongrel, joins in. When she sees the dogs the girl lowers her crossbow and reaches out her hand, making strange, whimpering noises at the back of her throat. Immediately the dogs stop barking and go down on their bellies, whining gently. At the same time she hears a door open in the hut and when she looks across she sees someone has lit a lamp inside which glows faintly through the small, dirty window.

'Shut up!' shouts a cracked voice from inside.

'Stinkin' vermin! Shut up or I'll put you back on those damned chains.'

The figure of a man appears in the doorway, the glow of a cigarette butt hanging from his mouth.

'What is it?' a female voice calls. 'Is it Caius back?'

'Nope.'

'Well, come in and shut the door, the baby's getting cold.'

The dogs stay where they are and the girl watches the door close. After a while she sees the shadow of a boy creep round the house from the other direction and slip in.

The cracked voice shouts and the baby begins to cry, wailing to such a pitch the girl can see Abel Dancer shaking his head to remove the noise. Then she hears the sound of a bottle hitting something hard and the door open as Caius leaves the house and makes his way towards them.

When the dogs see him they get up and creep to his side, their tails between their legs. Caius puts out a hand and strokes them, then slouches down onto the ground, his back up against an old dustbin. As the girl moves to him and touches him on the shoulder he jumps. Even in the dying light she can see a fresh bruise on his cheek.

'It's OK,' she says. 'It's me. From the woods.'

'You?' he says. 'Why are you here? Where's your bear?'

She gestures with her head to the trees. 'I've come to ask you something.'

'What?'

The door of the hut opens and the man staggers out, tossing an empty bottle into the trees. They see him climb into an old pick-up truck and start the engine, which chokes and splutters and eventually catches. The truck's headlamps sweep across the trees as he turns the wheel and, with a screeching of tyres, drives off.

'Is that him?' the girl asks. 'The man that made your scar?'

'I hate him,' Caius replies.

When the sound of the truck has gone the door opens again and a woman appears.

'Caius?' she calls. 'He's gone. Come back in.'

Caius gets to his feet. 'What did you want to

ask me?' he says to the girl.

'It'll wait,' she says. 'I'll still be here in the morning.'

The man in the truck does not come back that night. In the morning Caius comes out looking for her.

'Where's The Edge?' She appears from behind the pile of rubbish.

He picks up a stone and throws it at an old paper target pinned to a tree. 'It's just a rumour.'

'What does that mean?'

'They say that beyond the Green Wall is another place – The Edge. It's a kind of hell. Very dangerous. Wild. If you went there you'd be torn apart by crazy animals and heaven knows what else that might survive in there.'

But she is barely registering what he says. Her attention has been caught by the mention of the Green Wall.

'What's the *Green Wall*?'

Caius looks at her and scratches his head. 'Where have you been?'

She glares at him. 'Why do you keep saying that?'

'Well – you don't seem to know *anything*.'

'That's a stupid thing to say. I know lots of things. I know when a dog is ready to whelp. I know how to trap a squirrel. I know literally hundreds of things I bet *you* don't know about.'

Caius scuffs his feet in the mud. 'The Green Wall is the boundary.'

'Can you climb over it?'

Caius laughs. 'I shouldn't think so! I don't know.' His skin tone changes quite violently from pale pink to a very bright red. 'I've never been to it.'

'*Why haven't you*? Aren't you interested?'

He shrugs. 'You're not supposed to go near it.'

'Says who?'

'It's just a fact.'

'*Oh, facts*. Who cares about *facts*?' She bends down and tightens the laces on her boots. 'I saw that boy who trashed your net.'

'Really? What's he like?'

She shrugs. 'Oh, I dunno. He didn't hang

around. Have you seen the bear?' she says. 'My bear. I think he's gone looking for food.'

'Aren't *you* hungry?'

'Yes.'

Caius holds out a hand.

'Come and see my mother. She'll feed you.'

The girl has never held anyone's hand. She calls once more for the bear then pushes her hair back behind her ears and takes the boy's hand. It feels warm.

When they open the door the hut is dark and musty and it smells sour. There's an old sofa, a single iron bed and a table set for a meal. From the kitchen a woman appears with long, greasy red hair, a baby on her hip. She has the same pale, freckled complexion as her son.

'Who's this, Caius?' she asks.

'She's a friend.'

'Don't she have no name? Won't you introduce us?'

'She doesn't have a name.'

The woman eyes the girl up and down.

'Everyone has a name,' she says.

'Well, she don't.'

The woman shrugs and returns to her cooking pot. The baby starts whimpering and she jiggles it up and down on her hip.

'A girl that doesn't have a name,' she says and tickles the baby under the chin. She repeats her sentence, turning it into a little song. 'A girl that doesn't have – *a name* – she doesn't, doesn't have a *name*.'

The girl stands there awkwardly, wishing that Caius had not said anything. Although she's never thought of it before, at that moment the one thing she really wants is a name – anything to stop this woman singing.

'Shut up, Mum,' says Caius. 'Leave her alone, will you? I thought perhaps you could give her some food.'

'She'll need a name, son. We must give her one.' She turns to the girl.

'Your mama must have given you a name?'

'I don't have a mother,' the girl replies.

The woman passes the baby over to Caius and wipes her hands down her tattered apron.

'Where you from then?'

The girl remains silent and Caius's mother scans her face.

'You've got mighty pretty hair,' she finally says, touching the girl's head. 'Any ideas of what you'd like to be called?'

'I don't need a name,' the girl says.

'Well, we have to call you something. No name, eh?' She thinks for a while then bursts out laughing.

'Nona! What about Nona? See – No Name.' She laughs again and the girl shrugs her shoulders.

'I hereby name you Nona. Do you want some breakfast, Nona?'

The girl nods. The name sounds good to her ears and at least the woman has stopped singing that song.

Caius's mother tells her to sit down at the table and that she'll bring her some food. She tells Caius to set an extra place and, tipping out the contents of her saucepan, reveals something that looks like chopped meat but tastes of the riverbank. It tastes salty and bitter. If it had once been an animal, Nona thinks, it must have been pickled in its own tears.

'I'm Kath, by the way. You can call me Kath.'

The girl looks at her. 'Kath,' she says to herself. 'Kath. Caius. Nona.'

After breakfast the woman calls out for Nona to take a wash and she leads her into a small room curtained off from the living area and gives her a basin of warm water. Then she takes a brush and asks Nona if she can put it through her hair.

Nona watches Caius out of the corner of her eye, washing up the breakfast dishes and throwing a crust of bread to one of the dogs. She likes being in this house with these people but she can't stop thinking about the other boy and still feels anxious. Every tiny sound makes her inwardly jump. Somewhere outside is the man called Bolverk. She imagines what he must be like – some huge figure of a man with a cruel mouth perhaps, or maybe more like a snake who slithers into people's houses and squeezes them to death.

'Don't you have a home of your own, Nona?' Kath asks.

The girl shakes her head.

'Why not?' Kath tugs the brush through her hair.

'It's just a fact,' says Nona.

When she's finished with the brush Kath picks up a cloth and scrubs Nona's face.

'Do you have a father?' she asks.

Nona shakes her head and tells her that her father has died and that she is travelling north to find her relatives. Kath raises an eyebrow.

'Really?' she says.

Thinking of Thomas Bailey telling her not to lie, she changes her mind and tells Kath what has happened. She doesn't know that sometimes a lie can save you and if Thomas had been there he might well have pointed this out.

'So you have people after you, do you?' says Kath.

Nona nods.

'You can stay here a while if you like,' Kath says, her eyes narrowing like she's working something out in her head. 'But keep out of my husband's sight. I think it'd be better. He has a temper on him and I'd hate for you to get hurt.'

Nona looks at Caius's cheek, which has now turned purple and yellow, and nods.

Chapter 6

Abel Dancer keeps away from them. He feels threatened by the hut and the people inside. If he'd been able to speak he would never have told Kath the real story. He scavenges through the dustbins when Nona has gone and keeps his distance from the two dogs, which have now been chained up. Later, when Nona calls him, he is too far away to hear.

'Why did I leave him?' she curses, continuing to call out for him. 'I should never have stayed.'

Caius tells her that the bear will be all right – that he is a wild animal.

'But he's not!' she says. 'He's lived his whole life with humans. He hasn't developed the skills to survive out here.' Her face screws up. 'It's just a fact.'

Caius shrugs. 'You may have lost a bear but you've gotta name. You didn't have that before.'

Nona scowls at him.

The sound of a truck comes up through the woods and Caius stiffens.

'What's that?' says Nona. 'Is that your stepfather back?'

'Yes. You'd better hide somewhere, quick,' he says.

'But I've left my pack inside.'

She is cross with herself for feeling comfortable enough to leave the hut unarmed. Having a name is playing with her senses. It was bad enough losing the bear but to leave her pack was careless.

'I'll get it,' says Caius but they both know there is not enough time. The bonnet of the truck has come into view and Nona ducks down behind some bins.

A thin man with a grey face and hunched

shoulders gets out of the truck and spits. He ignores Caius. He has on a fancy pair of embroidered boots like a cowboy might wear and kicks one of the dogs as he passes by. He goes into the hut and immediately the baby starts to cry and Nona can hear a low murmur of voices. After about ten minutes, Kath comes out, climbs into the truck and drives off.

Nona feels uneasy leaving to look for the bear without her pack.

'Can't you go and get it now?' she whispers to Caius.

'If he's asleep I'll be able to. Usually if he's been gone all night he passes out on the sofa when he comes back. I don't know why Mum has gone, though.'

Nona thinks that the look on his face changes.

'When I've got your things, Nona, you should go. Something doesn't feel right.'

'Is that a fact?' she asks.

He disappears inside the hut and after a while he comes out, her pack under his arm. As he steps out of the door the cracked voice starts up.

'What you got there, son?'

Caius stops and turns round.

'Nothin', Dad. Just some stuff I found.'

There is silence for a few seconds and Nona feels her heart quicken.

'Bring it here. That looks like a crossbow you've got in there.'

She sees Caius hesitate for a moment as if he's going to turn back.

'No!' she shouts.

He looks behind him then runs out of the door towards her, throwing her the pack as he runs. It falls short of her just as the man appears at the door.

'What the hell's going on?' he says.

'I told you, Dad. Nothing.'

The man's eyes take in the fallen pack and the girl about to run and pick it up.

'Doesn't look like nothin', son.'

He hoists up his trousers and tightens the buckle on his belt, then runs his tongue over his dried lips.

'Who are you?' he calls out. 'You some thief or other come to steal from me?'

'No,' says Nona, stepping out into the yard. 'I don't steal. That pack is mine.'

'Bring it here, son.'

Caius stands his ground and watches Nona walk towards her pack and sling it on her back, taking the crossbow out as she does so.

'Oh, so you're going to kill me now, are you? Kath said she thought you were that kid that shot her stepfather.'

'I didn't shoot him,' she says.

'Oh, God!' Caius turns to her. 'That's where Mum has gone. She's gone to turn you in!'

Nona looks at him, confused.

'But why? She gave me a name. Why would she do that to someone she gave a name to?'

Caius shakes his head.

'I'm sorry, Nona. I'm really sorry. I never thought she'd go and do that.'

The man sneers. 'You're more of a fool than I thought,' he says. 'Do you know how big the reward is? Get her, Caius, or you'll be sorry you still live here.'

Nona turns to run just as a growling noise

comes through the undergrowth behind them. She knows the sound well. He prowls slowly out, his long back low to the ground, his jaw open. She marvels at his camouflage in the dappled light that comes through the trees. At the whiteness of his teeth. She remembers Thomas Bailey's words. *'If you put your hand up to defend yourself he'll have your arm. Then he will have the rest of you.'*

He comes from behind the man who has not seen him and when he springs at him the man falls forward, a surprised sound coming from his throat.

'Help me!' he screams. 'Get it off me.'

For a moment Caius stands staring as the leopard tears into the man, then he grabs the crossbow out of Nona's hand. She shouts at him not to do it and tries to wrestle it away from him but a shot rings through the trees and the leopard somersaults off the man and lies dead at his feet.

Kath stands in the yard, a rifle in her hand.

The man is writhing on the dirt, blood covering his face, his shirt ripped off his back. Nona grabs her bow from Caius as he stands, open-mouthed, staring at the dead leopard. Before Kath can turn the rifle on her she has it aimed at him.

'If you shoot me I'll kill your son,' she says, backing away. 'I trusted you. Why did you tell on me?'

Caius turns and blinks at her, a look of total surprise on his face.

'Nona . . .' he begins.

Kath puts down her gun and stares at her, her upper lip curling with disgust.

'I won't shoot you. You might be worth more alive.' She touches the leopard's stomach with the tip of her gun.

'They're coming for you now, Nona. You can run if you like but they'll get you. In the end you'll see there's nowhere to run to.'

Nona takes off back the way they came, over the stretch of moorland, the wind still thrashing across the tufts of grass and heather, towards the woods where she'd seen the boy. The rough terrain makes the going hard and she wonders if the weight of her name is slowing her down.

She keeps running, going over the events of the morning in her mind, not knowing how long she has before the trackers turn up. She could outrun them, but not their dogs. They wouldn't be like Caius's dogs – they'd be highly trained, fit and fast, and she doubts that they'd respond to her the way his did.

She can't see the bear anywhere.

After about five minutes she hears a fleet of vehicles driving up to the hut and, after that, faint barking. She reckons she has about an hour to set her trap.

Within half an hour she is back in the forest clearing. The net is where she'd left it, hanging on a branch, and she goes to work quickly.

The dogs are barely minutes behind her now.

With her knife she cuts several hardwood saplings, then she spreads the net out and makes triggers with the bent-over sticks. She pulls in broken branches to make a channel leading to her trap then covers the net with leaves, dead wood and mud made from the melted snow. She takes her crossbow out and stands waiting, the other side of the trap.

She has herself as the bait.

As she predicts, the dogs are quite a distance in front of the men and she hopes that once they've been caught in the net she'll still have time to vanish. She hears a crashing through the undergrowth towards her and tenses.

She expects the dogs to rush straight at her over the net, but what appears through the bushes is not the dogs. It is the bear, his crescent-moon shape stained purple with berry juice and his fur thick with burrs.

When the bear sees her he starts to rush towards her.

'Wah. Wah.'

'No!' she shouts. 'Don't come!'

But the bear does not understand her. He hears the word 'No' and hesitates a moment, then carries on moving, shaking and weaving his head and making small woofing noises. At that moment the dogs, hot on her trail, begin barking loudly.

Nona has made such a good channel to lead them to her that it is hard for her to skirt round the branches and broken bush to get to the bear and she can see her plan going terribly wrong. But Abel Dancer has heard the dogs too and his instinct is to run from them. He takes off just before he reaches the net and disappears into the woods.

The dogs come bounding up the path. Nona stands her ground, her crossbow behind her back.

There are only two of them and, just before they reach the net, they stop. They are still barking but she can see they have picked up the bear's scent and are undecided which direction to go in.

'Here!' she calls out. 'Come and get me. I'm what you want. I'm nice and juicy!'

With a leap, both dogs move forward, landing on the net, which sets the triggers off and immediately they are snarling and whining as the net closes around them and they are thrown up into the air.

Chapter 7

She has been running for about five minutes when the boy she'd seen earlier steps out into the path in front of her, blocking her way. Nona is not going to trust anyone and has her knife out in a flash. As she tries to dodge round him he catches hold of her arm.

'I'm not going to harm you,' he says. 'I'm going to help you.'

'Why?' Nona asks. 'You don't know me.'

'You're wrong.'

'How can you know me? I've never met you before – apart from yesterday.'

'If you'd like me to help you we must be quick. I can hide you for the time being. Follow me,' he says.

The boy turns away and in seconds disappears into the woods. Nona runs after him.

The path peters out at the edge of a quarry, which is overgrown with dock and the remains of nettles, now decaying in the winter cold.

'Quick – jump onto my back,' he says, stooping down.

'Why?' says Nona.

'Because you'll have a scent and the dogs will track it.'

'Well, then they'll follow *your* scent,' she replies, a hint of triumph in her voice.

'I don't have a scent. Now hurry up or they'll see us.'

She does as she is told and he carries her into the quarry, pushing past some tangled hawthorn, which reveals a shallow entrance to an underground space.

'Everyone has a scent.' She speaks from behind his back.

'You'll have to crawl in on your stomach,' he replies, ignoring her statement and letting her drop to the ground.

Nona does as she is told and scrambles in, followed by the boy, who pulls a door, camouflaged with brush and dead brambles, behind him.

The underground space is small and dark and smells of earth and roots. She wrinkles her nose in pleasure.

She turns to the boy who is crouching next to her and gives a start. All she can make out in the dark are a pair of yellow eyes, staring at her like a cat.

She is about to say something when they hear the noise of people moving through the undergrowth outside.

'You *are* special,' he whispers to her. 'You've got the chief of police out there – Bolverk. Did you notice a man in a leather coat?'

She shakes her head. 'I don't think so.'

He is peering through the gap in the door. 'Well, you've got to be someone important to get him out of his lair.'

She wants to tell him what has happened but how is she to know if she can trust him after what Kath did?

'Have you got a name?' she asks him instead. 'Everyone has a name.'

'What's that got to do with anything? Anyway – be quiet a moment until they pass by.'

'What if they don't – you know – *pass by*?'

The yellow eyes keep looking at her.

'They will. I've hidden here loads of times.'

Nona holds her breath, her ears straining for any sound outside their hiding place. All she can hear is her heart, beating loudly in her ears.

Her own eyes are getting accustomed to the dark now and she watches the boy withdraw his face from the door.

'Jay,' he says. 'My name's Jay.'

They crouch there, looking at one another.

'Aren't you going to ask *me* if I have a name?'

'What's your name then?'

'Nona.'

'Nona, eh? That's a pretty name. You didn't have that before. Where did you pick it up from?' He laughs.

She glares at him.

'Why would you say that? It sounds like you think you know me. But I've never seen you before. You said – didn't you? – that you've already met me.' She shifts her legs, which are bent awkwardly under her. 'Was it with Thomas Bailey?'

'Thomas Bailey – yes – I knew him. I remember him bringing you back – a snarling, snapping, feral thing. It was after the Big Cull. Covered in mud you were – your hair long and matted like you'd been living in a bush all your life. He said you probably had. He found you crying in some woods next to a female dog that had been shot. I wondered what he'd make of you.'

'I don't remember you.'

'You wouldn't. I left soon after.'

'Why?'

'Because of what he did to me.'

Before Nona can ask what he means, Jay puts a finger to his lips and turns back towards the door.

'They're still out there,' he whispers. 'You should have shot those dogs.'

'I'd never do that!'

'Well, they'll go back to Dissville soon, then we'll follow them.'

'Why?'

'Because it's the safest place to be right now! There's nobody out here. It will be less easy to spot you in a crowd – particularly if you're with the Circus, like me.'

'But I thought . . . Caius said you lived in The Edge!'

'The Edge? I wish! Is Caius that geek you were with who caught the leopard?'

Nona feels her cheeks flush.

'He's not a geek! A geek couldn't catch a leopard!'

'No, I suppose not. Sorry. I didn't know you cared so much.'

'I don't!' she hisses.

They sit in silence, then Jay takes something out of his pocket, a glass phial that has a thin brown liquid in it. He puts it in her hands.

'Drink that,' he says. 'It'll warm you up.'

'I'm not cold.'

'Then why are you shivering?'

Nona takes the phial and puts it to her lips.

'What is it?'

'Pochine,' he says.

She takes a swallow and pulls a face.

'It's burning my throat.'

'Like I said. It'll warm you up.'

Jay turns back to the door and rests his cheek against it.

'Why do you have this?' she asks.

'It takes away the pain. Come on – they've gone and it's dark out there now. We can at least get near Dissville before we hit the lights.'

'What does that mean?' Nona splutters, her throat still on fire from the pochine. 'Hit the lights?'

'They're all afraid of the dark! Dissville is always lit up. They think that evil lives in the dark.'

When they are sure that everyone has gone, Jay opens the door. He holds out a hand for her but Nona refuses to take it. They stand outside, straightening out their stiff limbs that have been bent for too many hours.

'I don't understand why we can't stay out here,' she says, looking up into the sky, which is littered with stars.

'Because they'll find you here. There's nowhere to run to. Anyway those choppers can't pick you out in Dissville. There are too many people.'

'That's what Kath said.' Nona steps away from Jay. '*There's nowhere to run to.* You're not like her, are you?'

'That woman with the red hair? Why would I be like her?'

Nona stares at him. His hair has fallen over his face, hiding some of his scars, but his eyes still gleam in the dark.

'Oh, no reason.' She hesitates. 'We can't go without my bear though.'

'He can come. He's over there – hiding in the bushes.'

Nona looks to where he is pointing and sees nothing but the outline of a few shrubs.

'How can you see that?' she asks.

Jay grins.

'I've got the eyes of a cat,' he replies.

It's not until the bear breaks his cover that she sees him for herself.

'Wah! Wah!' he says as she rushes towards him, her arms spread out.

'I remember that bear!' says Jay, a big smile spreading across his face. 'It's Abel Dancer, isn't it?'

The bear stops in his tracks, stands up and takes a few steps back.

'He doesn't seem to remember *you*!' says Nona, ruffling the bear's ears.

'He doesn't recognise me, that's why.'

'Why's that?'

'I don't look the same – *that's why*.'

The bear goes back onto his fours and Nona soothes him.

'What is it that happened to you?' she asks Jay.

Jay takes a deep breath.

'No one knows this. Only Dad and me, and now he's dead . . .'

'Dead?'

'There are wanted pictures of you all over Dissville, for the murder of my father – Thomas Bailey.'

Chapter 8

They set off towards Dissville, and in the last of the dark Jay begins to tell her about his father.

'I didn't kill him, you know,' she interrupts. 'I found him like that. Please say you believe me.'

'I believe you.'

'And I didn't know he had a son until just after – and anyway – they said . . . you'd been killed in a fire.' Nona frowns. 'Didn't death want you?'

Jay shrugs. 'I did die. *The old me.* Dad couldn't do anything for my mother but he tried – *something* – on me.'

He turns away, struggling to find the words

with which he could tell her what had happened to him.

'He was a scientist – did you ever go into his lab?'

She shakes her head, remembering the locked room she was never allowed into.

'So you *never* went into his lab? You had no idea what he did in there?'

Nona pulls a face. 'No. He told me once of an experiment he'd done on a baby monkey. He said he took it away from its mother and gave it the choice of a metal rod that had fur wrapped round it or a metal rod that had milk attached to it. He said the monkey always clung to the one which had the fur.'

She looks at Jay. 'We all choose to be comforted above our need for food. Whatever we are. Warmth and affection.'

He stares into the distance.

'Oh, he was always doing stuff like that. Messing around with animals.'

'And people,' Nona adds. 'He learnt from that baby monkey experiment, I guess. He was always kind to me and the animals, but I think he thought of me more as a project he could study. The animals always came first.'

Jay nods.

'He never told me why he was allowed to keep all those animals. I know he didn't have a permit for them,' Nona says.

'How do you know?'

'Some policeman came round.'

'A policeman? Oh, he wouldn't have known anything. Dad's work was top secret.'

'What was it then?'

Jay shrugged. 'Oh, just stuff. Inventions and things. He hated doing anything for the Authorities but I think they funded his work sometimes and he got to keep all his animals.'

They carry on walking in silence, then Jay stops.

'He liked to experiment when any of his animals died – he'd try and bring them back to life by giving them –'

He turns his yellow eyes to Nona.

'He *remade* me.'

'I don't understand. How could he remake you?' She frowns. 'Did he remake me too, do you think?'

Jay looks at her. 'I don't think so – unless you burnt to death in a fire.'

'So what did he do to you?'

'*He gave me a new heart.*'

Nona opens her mouth to say something but no words come out.

'When any of his animals died he kept their organs alive and used them on other animals. I suffered severe smoke inhalation – my heart had stopped. He said it was like I'd had a stroke. I couldn't move and I couldn't see.'

'What did he give you? Whose heart was it?' she whispers.

'He gave me *the heart of . . . a tiger*.'

Nona swallows, her own heart beating fast in her chest.

'It was a young tiger,' Jay continues, 'the first he'd bred in captivity. He loved it so much but one of the other tigers killed it. He kept its heart in ice.'

'What else? What else did he give you?'

'My eyes belonged to a cat. Some of my muscles come from a stag. I have leopard's blood running in my veins.'

'Oh my God.' She can barely speak now. '*Oh my God.*'

'So you see – I'm not really human at all. More of a . . . *creature.*'

They continue to walk towards Dissville – the bright lights now glowing in the distance. The shadows cast shapes on them and, for a moment, Nona thinks they look like stripes – tiger stripes across Jay's face.

'You said no one knew, but perhaps the Authorities funded it too, do you think? Do they know about you?'

Jay shakes his head.

'Is that why you're in so much pain?' Nona asks. 'Why you take that – what did you call it?'

'Pochine? Yes.'

Nona nods her head then begins to shake it. 'You're not a creature,' she says. 'You're – well, *different. Wonderful.*'

'My heart is in pain because I don't live a tiger's life. I'm trapped. Trapped in my body and trapped in the world I live in.' He touches the scars on his face as he speaks. 'And my limbs are in pain because I don't run like I should. A stag would leap and bound and jump. I can't tell you what it's like. Every morning I wake and, for a moment, I'm happy. Then I remember what I've become.'

'Why aren't you living in The Edge then? Like Caius said? Why are you still here?'

Jay shrugs.

'But you have a *tiger's* heart. Tigers aren't scared. They don't have a predator.' Nona frowns.

'Oh yes they do. And you know well what that is.'

'Man?'

Jay stares towards the lights of Dissville.

'Yes – man. But at the moment, Nona, they're after *you*.'

Nona watches the bear trotting in front of her and takes no notice of Jay's warning. 'We should all be living in The Edge. Why aren't we looking for it now? I don't want to take my bear back to people. I'm trying to get him used to being wild.'

'Yeah, but he can't really be wild. Not here. Look what they've done to where he'd live.'

Jay points out the stumps that had once been trees and the charred underbrush where acres of forest had been cleared away.

'No birds can sing here,' he says. 'We have to go to Dissville because you'll be safer there. We'll have to disguise you – maybe change the colour of your hair. If you stay with me in the Circus I'm sure you'll be overlooked. It's full of freaks and the few last remaining animals held in captivity. People love to come and see them.'

Nona's face turns down in disgust.

'But that sounds horrible!'

Jay stops and turns to her, raising his voice.

'Look. I don't think you realise what will happen to you if you are caught. No one's going to believe you didn't murder my father. You'll be put behind bars like all those animals at the Circus. Then you'll never be free.'

'But *you* believed me.'

'That's because I believe my father took his own life. After the fire and after my mum died he became depressed. You were a new project for him – someone who took his mind off things. If he thought they'd take you away from him he wouldn't have carried on. After I had gone you would have been all he had left.' He digs his hands in his pockets. 'I ran away shortly after he brought you home because I couldn't forgive him for what he did to me. He should have just let me die.'

He stops, opens his jacket and lifts up his shirt.

'Look. Look what he did.'

Nona stares at him. Long, red, jagged scars run around his torso. Angry-looking marks where he was stitched together cover his chest.

'I wish my heart would be pecked out by an eagle,' he says quietly.

'I'm glad he didn't let you die.' Her voice is soft. 'And please don't let your heart be taken. You must live for you both – you, and the tiger who lost *his* heart.'

Jay zips up his jacket and turns away.

'And I suppose you're right about your dad not wanting to carry on. Perhaps I meant more to him than I thought,' Nona says. 'He *did* tell me they'd threatened to take me into care. I wouldn't have let them though,' she adds, sticking her chin up. 'I'll do as you say for now, but I shan't stay long. I'm going to find where The Edge is. I don't want to live trapped in some place with people I don't know. The Edge sounds like somewhere we can be free – be *ourselves*.'

She stops and frowns. 'Caius says it's dangerous and wild – but I'm not afraid of that. I'm afraid of captivity.'

But in spite of all her courageous talk she still looks over her shoulder to check that Bolverk is not there.

The sky becomes brighter the nearer they come to Dissville, but a grey cloud hangs over the city.

'What's that?' Nona asks.

'Pollution from the power station,' Jay answers.

Nona nods. 'And that noise?'

'What noise?'

'That humming sound.'

'Oh, that. You know, I'm so used to it I'd forgotten it was there.'

'But what is it?'

'It's all the electricity. The generators – they buzz all the time.'

'This is going to drive me mad.'

Jay takes her arm. 'Like me – you'll get used to it.'

Nona sighs. She reckons that the people living here would never be able to tell day from night, spring from autumn. She is not sure she'll be able to stand it for long.

They stand on the brow of the hill and look down. The whole place is ablaze – huge arc lamps tower into the sky, hundreds of neon signs flash from buildings. Every window is brightly lit and a mass of people are moving to and fro under the streetlamps. Whole areas are illuminated by flood lights, where she can see people playing games and running round circular race tracks. *Nowhere to run to*, she thinks. It is a cold, greyish light; it doesn't twinkle, it doesn't glow – it just glares like radioactive fallout.

Looking at it, Nona longs for the darkness and to be cast back into the shade. She looks at Jay's face and his gleaming eyes as he stares down at

Dissville and she feels a warmth sweep through her body.

'Who are you?' she whispers to herself. 'Or rather – what are you?'

Whatever he was like before, he stands in front of her now as a beautiful and troubled soul, with an extraordinary power. Someone she wants to be with. Someone she can trust. Someone she could travel to The Edge with.

The bear doesn't like the lights either. He stands on his hind legs and dances around in a circle, weaving his head from side to side.

'What do we do with him?' she asks Jay.

'We'll have to leave him here for a while. I can come back for him, but right now if he's seen with you there'll be trouble. Will he stay?'

Nona is not sure, then nods. 'I'll leave my things with him. He'll know I'm coming back then.'

She takes off her backpack, looking longingly at her bow and arrows. She feels defenceless without them but if she left them she is sure he would stay. She looks at Jay, whose face is screwed up in pain. She has *him* though, she thinks, and she still has her knife.

She lays her things carefully on the ground and makes the bear lie down with them whilst Jay slips the glass phial from his pocket and takes a glug of pochine.

'Do you want any?' he asks. 'You know – for courage?'

Nona shakes her head.

'I don't need that stuff,' she says.

Chapter 9

When they reach the busy streets the lights are so bright they are almost blinding. As Nona's eyes accustom to the glare she sees the *Wanted* poster and tugs her hood down over her eyes whilst Jay grabs her arm, pulling her into a side street. It is an old picture of her that Thomas Bailey took a few years back, but it still looks like her. The green, almond-shaped eyes stare defiantly out of the poster, her long hair framing her pale face.

Jay hurries her along the brightly lit shop fronts, which are busy with people being served.

'Don't they sleep? It's the middle of the night!'

Nona says, her voice muffled in the fur of her hood. 'And look at them. They look dead, don't they? They all look so pale. And why are those children on *leads*?'

'Sssh!' says Jay in a low voice. 'Keep quiet. It's one of the laws. All children under the age of seven have to be harnessed.'

'Why?'

'In case they run away. You know, get an idea in their heads that there's a better place than this.'

'Why aged seven?'

Jay looks around him. 'They think after the age of seven children will have been filled with enough fear of the wild that they won't *want* to run anywhere! Hey – over there. It's him. It's Bolverk.'

Jay drags her into a doorway and puts his arms round her. She shrinks back against the wooden door as Jay presses against her, hiding her from view. She can feel his tiger's heart beating loudly through his jacket.

After a while he relaxes and she peers out from behind him, longing to see who she is supposed to be hiding from. In the distance she can make out a man in a black leather coat talking to two or three other men. He reminds her of a giant cockroach, encased in his black shiny armour.

She shudders. He has a broad, flattened body with spiny legs, and on his small head he wears long thin hair tied back in a ponytail. He turns his face her way and a light flares off a pair of wire spectacles.

'Ugh! He looks dead too. What's the matter with his eye?' she asks. 'It looks weird.'

'It's a cyber-eye. They say he lost the real one to a lion during the Cull and had a false eyeball fitted. It's a tiny camera. When he looks he can see and record everything.'

Nona shivers.

'Bolverk,' she says under her breath, 'I won't – I shan't – let you catch us.'

The Circus is even more crowded than the streets.

It's a large circular area with makeshift tents and cages and narrow pathways running zigzag through the mud. Nona peers into the cages, wondering if she'll recognise any of Thomas Bailey's animals that might have escaped the bullets and been captured. Most of them are in beast wagons, small trucks with barred sides that gave up travelling years ago. What few animals there are are either pacing up and down or just lying down looking bored. She stands in front of one of the cages. It houses a white lion who stares blankly out at her. His white coat is stained a dirty yellow, covered in scars, and his eyes are dull, with no spark of life in them. Eventually he yawns and turns away, swinging his head from side to side.

In one of the cages she sees a bear – larger than Abel Dancer – a big brown grizzly who stands up on his hind legs, bending his head as he reaches the top of the cage. Nona feels a lump in her throat. A group of kids are laughing at him and poking a stick through the bars.

'Stop it!' she shouts, marching up to them and snatching the stick out of their hands. 'How would you like to be poked with a stick?'

She jabs it at them. They back away in

astonishment and cry out for their parents. These kids are not on leads, and she wonders if they would behave the same way if they were.

Jay grabs the stick from her hand and pushes her under the flaps of one of the tents.

'You'll draw attention to yourself! Are you trying to be caught?'

'How can you just let things like that happen?' she says. 'They should be taught to be kind, not to be cruel.'

'This isn't your concern right now. We need to get you hidden.'

The tent offers some kind of relief from the lights but she can still hear the humming sound of the generators. Jay leads her over to a big trunk tucked away in a corner.

'I have to do a show now,' he says. 'I've been gone for too long. Someone will get suspicious. You'd better get in here and stay quiet.'

'When are you going to fetch the bear?'

'Later. When I'm done.'

Nona sighs. 'Well how long are you going to be?'

'Just wait here, OK?'

She watches Jay go back under the flap.

'What sort of show?' she shouts after him, but he has already gone.

Apart from the trunk, which when she looks inside is half full of dirty-looking clothes, there is a mirror and a table with sticks of make-up on and a clothes rail with a few tattered costumes. There is no one around.

She stares at herself in the mirror. She takes her knife out from her belt and grabs a hank of hair. She saws through it with her knife. Then she takes another piece and continues cutting until her long hair falls around her in the mud. Then she picks up a pot of white face paint and smears it over her face, adding a slash of red lipstick across her mouth. She smudges some black around her eyes and, taking off her coat, puts on a dress of sparkling black lace.

Out of the corner of her eye she sees someone crawl in under the flap.

At first she thinks it's a child but the more she looks the more she can see that it's an old woman – small, and dressed like a little girl in a short checked dress, white ankle socks and a tiny pair of red shoes. Her face is brown and wrinkled and she wears a lot of lipstick, which is roughly drawn around her mouth.

The woman nods her head at Nona, shuffles over to the trunk and removes a large overcoat. Then, without saying a word, she crawls back under the flap and is gone.

After a moment Nona follows her. The urge to see what Dissville is about will not let her hide in a trunk, and she's curious as to where the woman is going.

The narrow streets, which run through and round the Circus, are jam-packed with people. Although it's the middle of the night, it's so bright that Nona wants to shield her eyes from the light. The glare throws a deathly pallor over people's faces and accentuates the hollow shadows under their eyes. She spots the old woman who's now wearing the overcoat and who seems to have grown a couple of metres in height. She stares at her, wondering if she has suddenly gone mad. She had been so sure that the woman was no bigger than a doll. Is this a trick of the light? As she passes her she catches a glimpse of a tall, thin man hidden inside the coat and realises that she's sitting on the man's shoulders. Nona sighs with relief. She hasn't gone mad. Her awareness is all she has right now – that and her knife.

She walks by a boy playing a street piano with a monkey in a suit, attached by a length of chain. A man enticing a large snake out of a basket, a zebra being ridden bareback by identical twin girls, who are squabbling over something or other.

'Oh, shut up!' she hears one of the girls say. 'You're doing my head in!'

Nona walks on through the scrapping, shouting crowds, hating the noise and the bright lights and so many *people*. She passes the cage that housed the white lion. There is a man in there now, cracking a long whip. The lion breaks into a limping trot. In front of him is a ring of fire, which hisses and crackles and smokes. She knows that lions are terrified of fire and yet this poor creature aims himself at the hoop and jumps through the flames to applause from the crowd. The man cracks his whip again, touching the lion's flanks, and he sits down, swiping out with his big, heavy paw. Nona turns away, her eyes full of tears.

Further along she passes a crying child, who is being scolded by its mother.

'But I'm feeling sick,' wails the child.

'It'll be something you ate,' says the mother, tugging its reins. 'I told you to stop eating those sweets. *But you never listen, do you?*'

Nona feels sorry for the child and smiles at it but she is soon jostled towards another crowd, which has gathered round one of the larger cages. There's shouting and whistling and whooping and she has to push and shove her way to the front to see what they're looking at. When she reaches the cage she takes in a breath. There, prowling around, is a large female tiger and, sitting in the cage with her, is Jay.

At first she doesn't realise it's him. She sees a boy who has painted his body burnt orange and daubed black stripes across it. She watches him climb onto the tiger's back and wrestle with it to the ground. The crowd cheer and whistle some more and Nona watches, a feeling of joylessness and gloom sweeping over her body.

She turns away, finding the spectacle unbearable to watch and, as she does so, she spies Bolverk arguing with the boy playing the piano. She ducks down and tries to move away but the crowd is pressing on her from all sides and she is jiggled along, her feet barely touching the ground. She turns to look for Bolverk but he has left the boy and is out there, somewhere in the crowd. Now the girls on the zebra are riding through and Nona is pushed back towards the tiger's cage again. She tries to turn back but someone is blocking her way.

'You not enjoying what you see? The tiger boy and his tiger mother?' a hoarse voice whispers in her ear.

She looks up. It's the cockroach – Bolverk.

Chapter 10

Her instinct is to run but she's squeezed in. She looks into his face and into the eye of his cyber camera. His eye is a pale, glass-watery blue, like an icy pool of winter, and where the pupil would have been radiates a pinprick of light. She shudders.

'Excuse me,' she says, trying to get past him. 'I'm feeling sick. Something I ate.'

He stares at her.

'Too many sweets,' she adds, feeling the camera registering her face and the one thing that, when he watches the film back later, will give her away.

The green, almond shape of her own eyes.

The crowd lets out a scream and Bolverk's head swivels towards the cage. Jay has placed half his body inside the tiger's mouth and the tiger looks as if she's going to make a tasty snack out of him.

Nona pauses for a moment to watch but, seizing the opportunity, slips past Bolverk and, as if she'd become invisible, is lost in the crowd.

Most of the tents look the same and it takes her a while to find the one she'd been in. She runs over to the trunk in the corner and climbs in, covering herself with the clothes and praying that Bolverk does not follow her.

'We must go for the bear,' Nona says under her breath when she and Jay are back together. 'He can't wait there forever. Please go and get him.' She smiles sweetly at him. 'Perhaps we can do a little show, like you!'

Jay stares at her.

'We'll have to disguise that moon of his on his chest.'

'We can dye it like you said you'd do to *my* hair. You haven't said anything about my new cut. Do you like it?' She pats the back of her head.

'S'OK,' he says, wiping the paint off his face. 'Are you being serious about doing something with him in the Circus?'

Nona puts her hands on her hips.

'Oh, yeah! I'll teach him to jump through a hoop of fire! Course not! I'm not staying here, degrading myself like that. I'm going to find where the Green Wall is and get to The Edge. I'm not living like *this*. I keep saying we shouldn't be here – *but you never listen, do you*?'

'Wah! Wah!'

The bear runs towards Nona when Jay brings him back. She cuddles him.

'Where's my kit?' she asks.

'I've just hidden it in the trunk. Come on, I've got some brown dye from Esmerelda. Let's do you and him at the same time.'

'Did I tell you I bumped into Bolverk?'

Jay stops and looks at her. 'What happened?'

'Nothing.' Nona fiddles with the lace on the dress she is wearing. 'He just asked me if I was enjoying your show. Or rather – *not* enjoying it!'

'Well, I hope he didn't recognise you.'

Nona nods. 'Do you think he plays back the film he's taken?'

'Course. They say he does it as a ritual at the end of each day.'

'When would you say was *the end of the day*?' Nona asks.

She can imagine Bolverk sitting in front of a screen with her *Wanted* poster pinned to the wall. He'd know.

The dye is good.

Nona and the bear are transformed. When she looks in the mirror she thinks her hair looks like a beautiful shiny walnut.

'Thank you, Esmerelda,' she says to the little old woman who has helped her and Jay to apply the dye. 'Do you think anyone will recognise me?'

Esmerelda giggles. 'No, miss!' she says in a high-pitched voice. 'Not even your mother!'

Nona, Jay and the bear spend the night in the tent. Back in the trunk next to her kit, Nona falls into a deep sleep, dreaming of tigers and zebras and a large eye that shines down from the sky like the moon, casting a cold light over the land. And all the while she sleeps, the boy with the tiger's heart prowls around the tent, stopping to drink his pochine until he finally collapses onto the floor and shuts his cat's eyes.

Nona wakes in the morning with a feeling of dread. She knows that everything she imagined with Bolverk has happened.

He went back to his office in the early hours of the morning, removed his cyber-eye and plugged it into his computer. Keeping on his coat, he sat in a swivel chair at his desk and looked at the large screen in front of him. Occasionally he fast forwarded, stopping for a moment at the footage taken in the quarry where she and Jay were hiding and then forwarding it again until he was at the Circus. He had watched the act with the tiger a million times and was not interested in seeing it again. But when he bumped into her in front of the cage he stopped the film.

He doesn't know everyone who lives in Dissville but he does know when someone's face doesn't quite fit. This girl is interesting. From her make-up he assumes she works in the Circus. That black lace dress is hardly the clothing of ordinary citizens. She must be a new import. Perhaps from the North. The girl looks up at him for a moment then turns her head away. Her lips mouth the words, '*Excuse me. I'm feeling sick.*' He freeze-frames it and takes it back frame by frame till she's looking straight at him. He stares at the image.

Rifling through the papers on his desk he finds what he's looking for. A *Wanted* poster. For the murder of Thomas Bailey. Nona stares out of the picture at him. Her green, almond-shaped eyes almost daring him to catch her. He looks back at the screen, zooms in on her face and matches the eyes.

Chapter 11

'He knows it's me,' Nona says to Jay when he wakes up, yawning and stretching out on the floor next to her. 'I'm sure of it.'

Jay sits up and looks at her. She has been watching him sleep – he has tossed and moaned, his forehead damp with sweat. She wonders if the tiger-heart part of him is dreaming of a kill or the stag part of him of running and leaping towards The Edge. Two animals in conflict with each other within him.

In his sleep he'd murmured, 'What's your name? My name is Jay. What are you? I am just a boy.'

'I wouldn't think he'd recognise you looking like that,' he says.

Nona still has the white make-up plastered across her face and the black she'd smudged round her eyes now makes her look like a panda.

'But that's just it. I must get this off. He'll be looking for someone with white make-up on.' She looks at herself in the mirror and touches her head. 'At least my hair's different now.'

'Did you leave any stuff at Dad's? You know, any clothing or stuff you'd touched?'

'Yeah. I hardly took anything. Why?'

Jay gets to his feet. 'I don't think he'll come *looking* for you. I think he'll *smell* you out. He'll give those tracker dogs a piece of your clothing to sniff at and let them loose.'

'And there's nowhere to run to!' Nona says bitterly.

'Come here.' Jay holds out his hand to her. This time she takes it.

'You might not like this but I'm going to introduce you to my "tiger mother". You must rub yourself against her until every inch of you smells like a tiger. Dogs are terrified of tigers. They won't go near you.'

The tiger is pacing up and down inside her cage, covering the same path over and over again. They open the door and she turns towards Nona, growling at her, opening her mouth, revealing her magnificent teeth and swishing her long thick tail. Her muscles ripple through her coat and Nona shudders at the length of her claws.

'She's jealous!' laughs Jay, walking up to her and patting her neck. The tiger lifts her huge paw and puts it on his shoulder, nestling her head against him.

'It's OK, Mimi. She's a friend. Look – she's going to stroke you and you're to be nice to her.'

Nona watches the pair. There is a definite bond between them – two tiger hearts beating as one. First Jay gets a bucket and shovel and cleans her cage out, then he puts some food and fresh water in a couple of bowls.

When she's finished eating Jay takes Nona's hand again and leads her up to where Mimi is now lying, stretched out on the ground, licking her paw.

The tiger starts a low rumble in the back of her throat but, with Jay's encouragement, lets Nona rub herself up against her.

Smelling beautifully of tiger, Nona goes back into the streets of Dissville.

'Just don't look anyone in the eye, OK?' Jay says to her.

'But how can I tell what someone's like if I don't?'

'It doesn't matter right now. Your eyes are a giveaway. Just keep them looking down.'

'Oh, great! Then I won't be able to see anything.'

Jay relents and gives her a jacket with a huge hood.

'Stay inside that then!' He grins. 'Anyway, what can you really tell about someone just by looking into their eyes?'

'You can see their soul,' Nona replies.

'You can't see mine,' he says. 'Go on! Take a look.'

He pushes his face in front of Nona and tilts her chin up so that she can look at him properly.

'What do you see?'

She gazes into the yellow of his eyes. She can only see her own reflection looking back.

'Well? Can you see my soul?'

Nona shakes her head.

'No. I just feel I'm looking at a cat.'

'There! That's because *I don't have a soul*. My father forgot to put one in.'

'But that's ridiculous!' Nona protests. 'Everyone has a soul.'

'Well, I don't think I have.' He bites on his lip.

'Oh, you're doing my head in.' Nona puts the jacket on and disappears inside the hood.

'What do you remember before the fire?' she eventually asks.

'I don't remember anything.'

'Nothing at all?'

Jay shakes his head and pushes her back into the tent, spying a couple of Bolverk's henchmen who are demanding money from the man with the snake.

Once inside, he begins to pace up and down, round and round the tent.

'That's another of the things I lost – my memory.'

'But you've still got your own mind, haven't you?' says Nona.

'How do I know? If I can't remember what I was like before the fire I don't know if I have the same mind.'

'So, no memories at all?'

Jay shakes his head again. 'For God's sake, Nona, you do ask a lot of questions.'

'I want to know, that's all. You said you remembered *me* though.'

'Yeah I did. But you came after he'd done this stuff to me. And as I said, I didn't hang around for long after that.'

'But what was I like? Nona was persistent. 'You said you remembered him bringing me back?'

Jay sighs. 'You looked like a creature from the marshes. Your hair seemed black then, tangled with twigs and stuff, but your eyes – those weird green shapes staring out of a mud-caked face. You gave me the shivers.'

'That doesn't sound very nice,' says Nona.

'Well, that's the image I had of you. I only saw

your face though. When he brought you back he put you in a bag and tied it under your chin because you were kicking and scratching so much. And you made so much *noise*! You growled and barked when you saw someone and for the first few nights you howled and howled. And as far as I can remember you wouldn't sleep on a mattress. You used to curl up on the floor in a dark corner of the room.'

'I still don't sleep on a mattress.' Nona looks at the ground, a frown on her face.

'So how come you were brought up by these dogs anyway?' Jay says.

Nona shifts uncomfortably. 'Your dad could only tell me what other people said. About five years before he came across me, a young woman was found dead by the banks of the river. He reckoned she may have died in childbirth.'

'Was that giving birth to *you*?'

She shrugs and pulls at the sleeve of her coat. 'He said it could have been.'

'So . . . some dogs came to eat the afterbirth and found . . . *you*?' says Jay.

'That's what he said he thought happened. No one knew who the woman was or where she came from. They didn't bother to do any tests on her or anything.' Nona sighs and looks away.

'I'm amazed you survived. Hey – lucky the dogs didn't eat *you*.' Jay pats her on the back.

'He said he thought the female dog might have lost her own pups and picked me up and given me milk. I don't know. My memory has blocked out most of it. But I wouldn't remember that anyway, would I? I mean – you don't remember being born, do you? Or being a baby?'

Jay shakes his head.

'Sometimes I get flashes of things. It was quite a big dog family, I think. There was a lot of scrapping and playing around. We kept away from people.'

'Well, my dad did a fantastic job with you, didn't he? I mean – to teach you all those things. You know – *human* things.'

She nods.

'I suppose to teach me new things he had to teach me to let go of old things. I would never have eaten with a knife and fork. Or off a plate. Or worn clothes. He had to teach me to speak. Not just the words for things – I learnt that quick enough – but the *grammar* of things.'

They sit for a while, both lost in their own thoughts.

'And he taught me to be fair and considerate and not to judge, because he was all those things to me. I learnt to trust.'

She lapses into silence again.

'He did a fantastic job with you too!' Nona says eventually.

They look at each other, thoughts of their past lives flashing through their minds.

Jay shrugs. 'What else do you remember about your life as a dog?'

'I wasn't *actually* a dog. Well – I might have *thought* I was at the time. I never saw my own reflection. Sometimes I get flashbacks. I think I can remember the guns going off when they killed my dog mother in The Cull –'

Nona feels a lump in her throat like she's eaten something she can't digest. 'Thomas Bailey told me sometimes memory wipes things out that are very traumatic. Perhaps you're like me. Both of our memories are buried somewhere deep down.'

'Yeah. Actually, I don't really want to remember.'

'Nor me.'

Jay and Nona are now out on the streets again, leaving the bear eating a huge breakfast of nuts and berries that Jay had picked up when he'd brought him back to the Circus.

'You're a right pair, aren't you?' says Jay. 'You and that bear.'

'What do you mean?'

'Well, someone who is human brought up by animals, trying to learn how to behave like a human, with a bear brought up by humans who's trying to learn how to . . .' – as he speaks, his eyes are darting around the streets, checking on doorways and up on rooftops – '. . . be a bear! He has to learn to be in tune with Nature.'

Jay stops. Nona hears them too. Excited barks and howls.

'Bolverk's got the dogs out! Come on. Let's get out of here!'

They dodge round a corner, through a door into a house and out the other side. It is more crowded in this street and they push their way along the pavement, Nona clutching onto her hood to keep her face covered. She is beginning to feel panicky. There is barking in another street not far behind. It is Jay's description of being put away behind bars if she is caught that is filling her mind with terrible images, and she can't be sure the dogs will keep away from her tiger scent.

They try and get through another house but the door is locked and now they can see the men rounding the corner and coming their way. They dodge a food stall selling bowls of soup, accidently knocking into someone who spills the contents of their bowl on the ground.

'Oh, sorry! Sorry!' Nona says, but they cannot stop.

They keep running until Jay pulls her into a large tent, set back off the streets. They crouch by the entrance, catching their breath, and Nona strains her ears for the sound of barking above the hum of the lights, but outside it seems to be quiet now.

She is just relaxing when the sound of a gun goes off, somewhere behind them in the tent. She jumps and hides behind Jay, pulling him backwards into some people who have come in behind them. She can hear screaming from further inside and then another noisy round of ammunition, followed by cheering.

'What's happening?' she whispers. 'This makes me think of The Cull. When I was small.'

Jay points at a sign, which flashes out its message in large, red neon letters.

SAFARI

Nona thinks back to the night she ran away from Thomas Bailey's and the men who were talking about her and the dead animals.

'*Like going on safari, wasn't it?*' one of them had said.

'What is this place?' she asks Jay.

'You won't like it.'

She looks around. 'I don't like any of it,' she says. 'So you might as well show me.'

They follow a line of people through a door and they are immediately transported into a growling, snarling world where the lights have been dimmed. Nona is disorientated and clings onto Jay's sleeve, wondering where the animals are and why someone is handing out guns. Jay shakes his head at the man when he is offered one and they move on, pushing their way through an artificial undergrowth of shrubs and grasses. The sound of the animals seems to be coming from all directions and there is another noise, a high-pitched whirring that breaks through the chatter of the crowd.

'They've got the mozzies out,' says Jay.

'What are they?'

'They're there to create the atmosphere. Catch one and have a look – they're not real either.'

He swipes and claps his hands above his head and a tiny metal insect lies whirring in his palms. Nona picks it up.

'Careful,' says Jay, 'they can sting, you know. I think my dad had a hand in making these.'

She throws it on the ground.

'Why are they handing out guns?' she whispers, but before he can answer she sees a huge lion appear from behind a painted backdrop and the crowd around her scream. It moves jerkily towards them and Nona is struck by its strange-looking eyes that seem to be made of glass. A man next to her aims his gun at the lion and before she can knock the weapon out of his hand he lets off a volley of shot and is soon joined by others, shooting at a panther who has crept in.

'Oh, stop it! Stop shooting!' she shouts, but Jay has his hand over her mouth. Seconds later something swings down from the ceiling and flies over her head. More guns go off. She looks up to see a large chimp on a wire.

'What's happening, Jay? I don't understand.'

'Safari,' he says grimly. 'They get the thrill of the kill but really there is no danger. It's animatronics. Those animals have been stuffed.'

Nona stares at the chimp in horror and feels the tears welling up inside.

She buries her head into Jay's chest, afraid that people will notice her crying.

'Is that what they've done to all Thomas's animals, do you think? Have they stuffed them too?'

Jay nods. 'I expect so. Come on. Let's get out of here.'

They get out into the streets once more, where Bolverk's men are still loitering. They walk briskly away, dodging in and out of tents. Nona has stopped looking where she is going, bumping into people as she hurries along beside Jay. She is just rounding a corner when she walks smack bang into a boy walking the other way.

'Watch out,' says a voice.

Nona peers out from inside her hood. It is a voice she recognises.

It is Caius.

'Caius!' she says, lowering her hood. 'It's me! Nona!'

Chapter 12

Caius takes a step back and looks at her closely.

'Nona? Is that really you? It doesn't look like you! What's happened to your hair?'

'Ssssh!' says Jay. 'Keep your voice down.' He pushes them both up a side alley, pulling Nona's hood back over her face as he does so.

'Hey – what's going on?' says Caius.

'Tell you in a minute,' whispers Nona.

The men that they saw earlier pass by without looking in their direction and Nona relaxes.

'Hey, Caius – this is the crazy person you told me about. The one who let the leopard go.'

The two boys glare at each other, shifting awkwardly on their feet.

'Yeah, I used to watch you sometimes,' says Jay. 'Some of your traps were rubbish!'

Caius is about to say something but Nona grabs his arm.

'I've cut my hair shorter and now it's brown.'

Caius nods. 'So I see. I've also seen those *Wanted* posters of you.'

'Yeah. They're doing my head in. I don't look the same though, do I?'

Caius shakes his head, eyeing Jay as he does so.

'Anyway – what are you doing here?' she asks.

'Well – I've – I've left home. It was bad what my mother did.'

Nona nods, noticing for the first time that he has a split lip.

'Look, Caius,' she says. 'That thing with the bow and arrow. I wouldn't have killed you. I hope you know that. I just couldn't think what else to do.'

Caius stares at her.

'So,' she carries on, 'why are you *here*?'

He blushes, a bright red flush, which spreads over his face.

'I – I – well – I came to look for . . . *you*!' He looks down at his feet.

'Come on, Nona – this is dangerous standing here,' says Jay, pulling at her sleeve and trying to get her to move.

'I wanted to know if you'd got away. I reckoned I'd find out here.' Caius raises his eyes and looks her in the face.

At that moment some dogs appear at the end of the alley, straining on their leashes.

'Quick.' Jay tugs on Nona's arm. 'We must go.' He turns to Caius, almost tucking Nona into his coat. 'See yer!'

Walking fast, Jay and Nona make their way back to the tent.

'What's *he* doing here?' Jay mutters in her ear.

'He told you! He wanted to know if I was safe.'

'We don't need him with us. He'll get in the way.'

But Nona disagrees. 'He's fine. He was kind to me.' She turns to see where he is and he is following a few paces behind them.

When they enter the tent, they see that Esmerelda is sitting at the dressing table, crying silently.

In their absence, everything inside the tent has been turned upside down. The trunk where Nona had slept is tipped over in the mud, the black lace dress she wore is torn to threads.

'I didn't say a thing,' Esmerelda splutters. 'Though they tried to make me. I said I didn't know anything about you and I didn't know where you'd gone. I kept you out of it.' She turns to Jay. 'I didn't want anything to happen.'

'Was this Bolverk?' Jay asks.

'Yes – Bolverk, and his men.'

'Where's the bear?' says Nona in alarm.

'He's gone!' Esmerelda's little face looks downcast. 'He ran away when he heard the dogs coming. I don't know where he is.'

'I'll get him!' Caius is standing at the entrance to the tent. 'He can't be difficult to find. I'd like to be useful,' he adds.

Nona nods at him and turns on Jay. 'Oh, why did I come here? You were wrong. This is no safer than where I was before.'

Jay looks on, a pained expression on his face, his hand in the pocket of his jacket. Nona knows it is clutching the phial of pochine.

'The bear's lost his moon,' says Nona to Caius, picking up a discarded sweet she sees in the mud. 'We dyed it brown, like my hair. Here – give him this sweet if you find him. But hurry. They'll capture him too if they see a bear on the loose.'

'Where do you think he'll be?' says Caius.

She thinks for a moment. 'Look for fizzy drinks! I bet he's found some.'

Caius runs out of the tent as Jay slumps down beside the upturned trunk.

'Listen, Jay,' says Nona, kneeling down beside him. 'Let's get out of here, OK? After this I can't stay anyway, Bolverk will find me. We'll travel until we find the Green Wall – then somehow, however hard it is, we'll be on the other side and we'll be free.'

Jay's eyes scan her face, his hand reaching into his pocket to touch the bottle of pochine. 'OK,' he says eventually. 'I'll come with you.'

* * *

When Jay goes to Mimi's cage he sees the dogs sniffing around it.

He hangs back and watches Bolverk talking to some of the Circus people. He can see them shrug and shake their heads. No, they have never seen a girl fitting Nona's description.

'Do you think the tiger got her?' He hears one of the men ask Bolverk. Bolverk doesn't answer and takes a sweet out of his pocket, screwing the paper up and throwing it onto the road, where it soon gets trampled into the mud.

'We've done here!' he says to the dog handlers. 'We'll check out the houses now – someone is hiding her.'

The boy who plays the piano slithers up to Jay, his monkey grinning wickedly.

'Hi, Crow,' says Jay.

'You want some more pochine?'

Jay shakes his head.

'That girl wot you've got hangin' around. Who is she?' he says.

Jay shrugs. 'Which girl is that?'

'You know which girl.' He is grinning like his

122

monkey now. 'Short brown hair and weird eyes.'

'Oh, that girl. She just latched onto me. I don't know who she is.'

'Funny that there's lots of interest in a girl and then *she* turns up.' He scratches his armpit. 'Do you think she's anythin' to do with that bloke wot they found murdered? You know – like on the poster?'

Jay frowns and tries to stroke the monkey, which bares its teeth and chatters in Crow's ear.

'Do *you* think she looks like the girl on the poster then?' Jay asks.

Crow shakes his head.

'Nah. Maybe not. But then – maybe she does. There's a reward, you know.'

Crow takes a sweet, which he's been given, out of his pocket and slips it into his mouth, sliding his tongue around it and making loud sucking noises.

'Yes, I know, but that girl's harmless enough. In fact, between you and me,' Jay lowers his voice and moves his mouth as near to the boy as the monkey will let him, 'I think she's a bit simple.

You know – something wrong in the head.'

Crow looks surprised and nods.

'Well – just watchin' your back, mate. You know where to come when you need any more . . . you know.' Then he tucks the monkey under his arm and wanders over to his piano again.

Jay runs back to the tent, where to his annoyance he sees Nona talking with Caius, who has still not found the bear. He hangs back. Caius is showing Nona a leaflet he's picked up, advertising the Circus.

'Look,' he says. 'There's a picture of Jay and a tiger. It says: "*Go see the show. This boy has a savage grace.*" What on earth does *that* mean?'

Nona shakes her head.

'Hey, that stuff Jay drinks. What is it?' Caius asks.

Nona shuffles her feet and pulls at a loose thread in her coat.

'Um. Pochine, I think.'

'Why does he drink that?'

'I dunno. Some sort of pain.'

'What's happened to him? Has he had some accident?'

124

'Yeah. Maybe.'

Jay, seeing Nona struggling with the truth, pulls back the tent flap and goes up to her.

'Give me something of yours that doesn't smell of tiger,' he says. 'We've got to do something. There's too much interest in you.'

'All of me smells of tiger!'

'There must be something.'

Nona's eyes brighten.

'My backpack, I suppose. I wasn't wearing that.'

'Well, give it to me quick.'

'Why? What do you want it for?'

Jay ignores her and takes the pack from her hands, turning to Caius as he does so.

'Where do you think the most dangerous part of Dissville is?'

Caius shakes his head. 'I dunno. The power station, where they generate all the lights? I hate that horrible place. I think it would be easy to be burnt alive in there.'

'Good,' says Jay. 'That's what I think too.'

He does the pack up and turns to Nona.

'So there we are then.'

'What are you going to do with my backpack?'

'I'm going to leave a false trail. Those dogs want a scent to follow and we've cheated them of one. If I lead them to the power station and chuck in your bag they may think you've been killed in there and leave you alone.'

'Brilliant!' says Caius.

'But that's my backpack! What am I going to carry my stuff in?'

'We'll find you something else.'

'Well, I want my bow and arrows.'

Chapter 13

Leaving Caius to look for the bear they start the trail from behind Mimi's cage. They walk along the streets, stopping by lampposts and rubbing Nona's pack up against them, all the while checking over their shoulders that no one has seen them. High up on a lamppost a monkey in a suit watches their departure then scampers back over the rooftops to chatter in Crow's ear.

They get to the outskirts of Dissville and head off towards the power station, a loud, electrified area full of noise and generators, pushing and pumping and charging live currents through wires and cables. Jay has never been there, always keeping clear of the skull posters and their prediction of immediate death.

Nona is deep in thought.

'I've never understood why they had to kill everything,' she says. 'Why they had to kill my dog family. What harm were the dogs doing?'

'Things have got worse over the years. My dad said they cut down the trees because the Authorities thought the woods and forests were places to be feared. Where dangerous animals lived, where dangerous *people* could hide.'

'What sort of dangerous people?'

'Oh, people who had committed crimes, I guess. Anyway, that was long before you or I were born. When they started cutting down all the trees, the animals lost their homes. Some of them became vicious, but not all. But they shot them anyway. Or captured them. Those that were left began to adapt.'

Jay thrusts his hands in his pockets. 'My dad said that a new government department had been set up even before *he* was a child that was responsible for people's safety. But it got out of hand. They passed so many laws that soon nobody was allowed to do anything without a government permit and those animals – well, *they* didn't get permits, did they?'

'Was it Bolverk who ordered The Cull?'

'I don't think so. He's only the chief of police. But he's the face of the Authorities. They give him orders and he carries them out. The Authorities don't have any contact with *real* people. They all sit behind walls and make the laws. If you put fear into people they're easier to control. That's what my dad said.'

Nona thinks of Bolverk.

'Yes – and if you give people power . . .'

Jay pulls a face. 'Yeah. 'Specially if you give the *wrong* people power.'

Nona remembers back to the time before she'd ever even heard of Bolverk, let alone seen him. She hadn't been afraid then.

'They knew about me, didn't they? Those people making the laws?'

'Yes. I guess they did. They knew about you

when Dad had you. I'm amazed they never caught you before he found you.'

'They nearly did! I do remember *that*. It was just before my family were killed. They were older boys. They came down to the river to fish and I was hiding under the bridge. I'd strayed off, which I knew I should never have done. When they saw me they started shouting and threw stones at me. Instead of running away from them I ran towards them. I wanted to get them back for hurting me. I tried to bite one of them but the rest of the pack came and dragged me away before I could go after him.' She pauses, then, taking a deep breath, continues.

'We had to hide a lot after that. Those boys came out looking for us.'

'So. You do remember some things,' says Jay.

Nona nods and realises her heart is racing with the memory.

As they near the electrified perimeter fence, Jay's heart too begins to beat louder and louder, sending its own electric impulses through his body. He can hear it beating in his ears and shakes his head to try to get rid of the noise.

'Aargh!' he groans, doubling up and falling to the ground. His head is throbbing like an engine contained in a small box, sending signals to his eyes, which feel as if they're burning holes in his face. His veins seem on fire. His muscles are expanding.

Suddenly he convulses and rolls over, dropping the backpack he has been so carefully holding. Nona steps back in alarm. His legs bend up underneath him in a foetal position. He hugs them to his chest, moaning and crying like a newborn, his body shaking.

'What's your name? My name is Jay Bailey. What are you? I am just a boy.'

'Jay!' cries Nona. 'What's the matter? What's happening to you?'

But now Jay can't speak. His yellow eyes are wide and unseeing. He feels as if he is being ripped into a thousand little pieces.

She drops down onto her knees in front of him and touches his hand. A huge surge of electricity shoots through it and enters her body. She yelps and drops his hand.

'Jay! Say something. What can I do?'

Foam is now coming out of his mouth and mixing with the earth, where it fizzes and bubbles. Nona grabs him by his coat and begins to pull him back, wanting to get him clear of the area. Caius's image of being burnt alive is in her mind.

He is surprisingly light and she manages to drag him across the ground until they are far enough away from the perimeter fence for him to stop convulsing. But he has begun to tear at his coat, ripping open his shirt to expose the angry-looking scars, which are now spouting blood. His skin looks raw and thin and Nona can see his veins and arteries pulsing through his chest. It frightens her and she moves away, afraid that he will not recognise her and lash out.

He suddenly stops shaking and lies there, staring up at the sky.

'What happened?' says Nona, keeping her distance.

Jay's words are slurred.

'The fire. My mum. We are trapped in one of the barns. It sweeps through the building so quick. The flames. Like red and yellow fingers.

'There are no windows. The door is jammed. It's OK, Mum. It's OK. The door isn't opening. Please don't cry.' His eyes flicker and his face screws up in agony.

'The smoke! I can't breathe. I can't breathe.' His head thrashes on the ground and his eyes open in alarm.

'You can breathe, Jay. You're not there any more. You're with me.' Nona moves to kneel next to him. She strokes his head and his eyes close.

'I'm on a table. My father is looking down at me. I have wires – hundreds and hundreds of wires running all over my body. I can't breathe. Oh – the smoke.' Jay starts to pant, clutching his throat.

'I can't breathe. I can't breathe.'

He sits up for a moment, then drops back onto the ground.

'I don't know what's happening. Why's there a mask over my face? He's flicking a switch. My body's on fire again. Electricity pumping through me. Stop it! Please stop it.' His hands claw the ground in pain but he carries on remembering.

He clutches Nona's arm.

'My heart starts beating loudly. I can feel blood running through my veins. My muscles twitch. My limbs are jolting. Jerking and dancing on the table. Every fibre in my body hurts.' Jay pauses for breath.

'That's how he gave me life.'

Jay lies where he is on the ground for a long time, his eyes shut.

He is still now.

Nona curls up next to him and takes his hand again. This time there is no shock. She strokes it.

'You shouldn't blame him,' she says. 'He did it to save you. Because he loved you.'

They lie together, saying nothing.

Nona is shivering now and Jay rubs her arms.

'Nona?' he says.

'What?'

'Do you wish you were still with the dogs? That you'd never learnt to act like a human?'

She frowns. 'I can't really answer that. After all – I didn't have any choice. Do you still wish your father had let you die?'

Jay looks at her and slowly shakes his head.

'Well, there we are then,' says Nona.

Then she walks over to where he dropped her pack and hurls it into the centre of the power station. It catches on one of the cables, which buzzes and sparks, and the pack jerks and jolts like Jay's limbs stretched out on the table.

Chapter 14

'I still haven't found the bear, but I know where the Green Wall is,' Caius announces on their return.

'But . . . but you said you'd never been to it! Is this a kind of trap?' Nona looks at him, her mouth dropping open, her face full of suspicion. 'Perhaps you're like your mother after all.'

Caius's face flushes.

'I know I said that, but it's not a trap. I have been there. Ages ago. I didn't tell you because you're not supposed to go near it, and I didn't want to be found out.'

'Where is it then? What's it like?'

'It's north-east of here,' Caius replies. 'I found it by chance one day when I was out hunting for rats.' Caius shifts his feet. 'Everyone is always told not to go near it. That if you're found close to it you'll be carted off to prison.'

'But that's stupid!' says Nona. 'You can't be imprisoned for just looking at something.'

'Yes you can. Here you can, anyway. So I don't go round telling just anyone that I've seen it.'

'Can we get over it?'

'I don't know. It's high and there are snake pits.'

At the thought of this, Nona shudders. 'I didn't think there were any snakes left. Can they get out?'

'No. They are all wired in,' says Caius. 'But there are hundreds of them, slithering and sliding everywhere, and most of them are enormous. Everyone knows that. Some bite and some are poisonous. You'd have an agonising death as the poison went through your veins and your heart would stop and you'd turn purple. If you weren't poisoned or bitten to death other snakes would wind themselves around your neck and *strangle* you to death and your eyes would pop out.'

Nona shuddered.

'A timber rattlesnake's venom destroys your blood vessels, and even if you were fortunate enough to survive the initial attack, lasting damage often occurs,' Caius carries on, speaking as if reciting from a school book.

Nona's mouth hangs open. 'Yes, but even if they're wired in we'd still have to cross over, wouldn't we?'

Caius nods.

There is a scrabbling at the back of the tent and they turn to see the bear's nose pushing under the flap.

'Yes!' says Nona as the bear's head appears, followed by his large body. There is a ripping sound and the tent shakes and wobbles. She runs over to him and hugs him.

'Well, what are we waiting for? We'll sort the snakes out when we get there, won't we? Why don't we go now?'

'Because you're still being hunted. We should

wait to see if our trick at the power station has worked,' says Jay. 'And also there are some things we'll need. We'll need some rope and we must travel at night. It won't be easy leaving with a tiger and a bear.'

'Oh!' says Nona, looking shocked. 'Are you planning on bringing Mimi?'

'Of course. I couldn't leave her behind in a cage for the rest of her life. Come on, Caius. I need some help.' He turns to Nona. 'You'd better stay here.'

She watches them walk into the streets and sighs. She sees Jay stop and speak to Caius then point up at something moving along the rooftops. He shouts at Nona.

'What?' she shouts back, but their voices are lost in the crowd. The girls on the zebra ride past her, blocking her view, and when they've gone Jay and Caius have gone too.

She waits for a while, then she goes back inside the tent. She does not notice Crow, who is watching her from behind his piano.

The bear is sleeping, lying flat out on the floor,

tied up to one of the tent posts by a piece of string. He is snoring gently. She wonders where he's been and is about to go over and lie with him when she hears a noise coming from inside the trunk. As she walks over, a monkey pops his head up from underneath the pile of clothes and bares his teeth at her.

'Oh, it's *you*,' she says, stretching out her hand to stroke him. The monkey makes a little screaming sound and jumps out of the trunk, then runs round the tent and swings himself up into the rafters.

'Come on down!' Nona cries. 'I won't hurt you.'

But the monkey stays where he is, squawking loudly.

'You got my monkey?' Crow says, coming into the tent.

Nona stares at Crow. He's small and wiry and it crosses her mind that he looks very similar to his monkey. Not in his clothes, mind – the monkey is dressed in a sharp suit and this boy has tight trousers and big boots and wears a bowler hat. But there's a definite likeness. Even his fingers are long and thin and look as if they could curl round a branch and swing him up into the trees.

'You're the boy who plays the piano, aren't you?' she says.

Crow nods and gives her a grin.

'This your bear? I've never seen you do anythin' with it. You new round here?'

Nona nods. 'Yeah. But I'm not staying.'

'Oh, really?' Crow beckons to his monkey, who jumps down from the rafters and sits on his shoulder. 'Where you off to then?'

'For God's sake. You ask a lot of questions,' Nona says.

'What's wrong with that? Only interested. We don't often get newcomers. I wondered what brought you here.'

Nona looks at her stash of arrows and her bow awaiting a new pack and decides not to tell him anything. Instead she asks him if he's been to the safari.

'Yeah – but what's that to do with anythin'?'

'Just wondered what your monkey thought of all those stuffed animals.'

'Well, hey! I've never asked it. Do you think I should?' He turns to the monkey. 'Now listen here, Micky. Got any thoughts on that chimpanzee in the safari? No? Didn't think so.' Crow turns to Nona. 'He doesn't have an opinion on that. But he does have an opinion on somethin' else though.'

'What's that?' Nona asks.

'He thinks you look like that girl in the *Wanted* poster. Same eyes, see.'

Nona's heart misses a beat.

'I've not seen a *Wanted* poster. What's this person supposed to have done?'

'Oh, just killed someone. You oughta go and take a look.'

Sensing that all is not right, the bear struggles to his feet and makes a growling sound in his throat.

'That bear safe?' Crow asks as he backs towards the edge of the tent.

'No,' says Nona, undoing the string. 'I think he could take your arm off. Perhaps you'd better be leaving.'

Crow doesn't wait to be told twice and, with

Micky bounding off in front of him, he runs from the tent.

She tells Jay and Caius about his visit when they come back.

'Crow?' says Jay.

'Is that his name?' asks Nona.

'I saw his monkey up on top of our tent when we left. I should have realised Crow wouldn't be far behind. Did you tell him anything?'

'Um – like what?'

Jay puts down the bags he's carrying. 'I don't trust that boy. Did he get a good look at you?'

'He said he thought I looked like the girl on the poster. Well, actually he said the monkey thought I looked like the girl on the poster.'

Jay looks at Caius and raises his eyebrows.

'He knows it's you. This is bad news. We should get ready to leave tonight.' He beckons to Caius. 'Come and help me sort out Mimi. And, Nona, I've got you some warmer clothes that you should get into. We've no idea what it'll be like the other side of the Green Wall.'

They go to leave. 'Oh, and, Nona?' he says again. 'Secure the bear, will you? We don't want him running off again.'

They go out through the back and Nona picks up the string to tie the bear up but before she can get it round his neck he has gone up on his hind legs, danced a little jig and disappeared under the tent flap.

Nona cries out for him to stop but when she looks out from under the flap he has vanished.

Chapter 15

'Where's the bear?' she asks the boys when they return.

They look at each other.

'Dunno,' says Caius. 'He didn't come with us.'

'But he did!' says Nona. 'He ran out after you.'

Jay says they'd better go and search for him and a worried look crosses his face. 'They'll catch him this time, Nona.'

'Well, I'm coming too. He knows me.'

They search the streets, Nona keeping her head down as best she can. As they near the safari tent she sees him.

'There he is. Look!' She points him out to Jay but the bear has already disappeared round the back of the tent.

'Oh, no,' says Jay. 'He's gone inside. This is bad news.'

They both have the same thought and run towards the tent.

The noise seems even louder than before as Jay and Nona push their way inside. They go through a door, a combination of gunfire and screaming filling their ears. They find themselves backstage, behind a painted cloth depicting a jungle scene. Above them swings the chimpanzee and, this time, Nona can see he's attached to a zip wire which takes him out into the main tent.

They push themselves around the backcloth and, to their horror, find themselves on the stage area, facing hundreds of people with guns. In front of them is the lion with a huge bear on its back.

'Oh my God! Don't shoot it – please don't shoot the bear!' Nona screams.

'That bear's for real!' she hears someone shout and the crowd shrinks back from the platform.

The lion is now lying on its back, its stiff legs pointing upwards, and the bear is gnawing on its neck.

There's a shot and the bear lifts his great head in surprise and stares at the crowd. Then another shot is fired and another.

'No. No, please!' Nona is crying now and Jay is trying to get her off the stage. Everyone who is not shooting at the bear looks at her.

Jay whispers in her ear that the bullets are duds.

'He'll be OK if we can catch him. But not in front of all these people. If it gets back to Bolverk he'll know it's you. Come on – quick!'

Jay bundles her outside.

'Let's go round the back where he got in.'

As they rush round the side of the tent they see Crow and the monkey standing in the street.

'Your bear's in trouble,' Crow says to them as they pass. 'Won't be long now!'

'What does he mean?' Nona whispers to Jay.

'Oh, who cares? Look, he's over there – coming towards us.'

Nona runs and grabs him by the ruff of the neck.

'Oh, Bear! You are so bad. So bad.'

People are now crowding out of the tent, still screaming, which agitates the bear, who goes up on his hind legs and starts a sort of jig.

'We've got to get him out of here.' Jay is pulling at Nona's sleeve now. 'You go – back to our tent. I'm going to take him. He can wait for us with Mimi. Then tonight we'll leave.'

On her way back to the tent Nona sees Caius standing in front of one of the cages. She watches him from a distance to see what he's going to do but he appears to be in a trance, his eyes fixed firmly on whatever is inside. She goes up to him and sees he is looking at the white lion.

'I feel so sorry for that animal,' he says when Nona touches his arm.

'Why do you think a creature like that jumps through those horrible hoops of fire?' Nona asks.

'Because he's afraid,' Caius replies. 'He's more afraid of the punishment than actually jumping through the fire. Look at his scars. He's been hit a lot I'd say.'

Nona nods. She has found all the caged animals

a distressing sight and can't wait to leave. 'I'm going back to the tent to pack. Are you coming?'

Caius shakes his head. 'I'll be along later. I think I'm just going to stay here for a while.'

She leaves Caius and returns to pack her things. There is no one else there so she starts to gather up a few bits and pieces, unaware that outside, Bolverk and two of his men are pushing Esmerelda roughly in front of them towards the tent.

Nona has her back to them and is carefully putting her bow and arrows into a new pack that Jay has found for her. She has let her guard drop and is not listening. The first she is aware something is wrong is when the monkey leaps onto her shoulder and starts pulling her hair.

'So, we meet again,' says Bolverk. 'Or shall I say we finally have you!'

Nona turns around, pushing the monkey off her neck. It leaps onto Crow, who is standing just inside the tent.

'We thought for a moment you'd been burnt alive at the power station. Nice little trick that. But people who play tricks get punished.'

Nona's mouth has gone dry and her heart is beating so fast now that she finds it hard to speak. She swallows.

'How did you know? That I hadn't – er, burnt?'

She starts to back off, measuring her chances of making a dash for the back flap and getting away.

'Just call it instinct. Like I've got a third eye!' he chuckles. 'You've led me on a merry dance. A bit like that bear of yours, I think.'

He gestures to the men as Nona makes a grab for her bow and arrows, but she is too late.

She is dragged away, biting and kicking, and bundled into the back of a truck where three of the search dogs lie crouched. When they see her they shrink back, the smell of tiger too much for their quivering snouts.

When Caius returns, he finds Esmerelda on her hands and knees, moaning to herself as she tearfully tries to collect a trail of sweet papers littered in the mud.

Chapter 16

Her cell, which is small and grey, has bars just as Jay had told her, and no windows.

'I haven't done anything – please believe me!' she says to one of the guards who pushes her in.

He laughs at her. 'They all say that.'

'But I haven't. I loved Thomas – I'd never hurt him. Jay believes me and he –' She stops short, not wanting to involve him. But the guard is not listening.

'Bolverk will fill you in on what's going to happen to you.'

Nona wails, 'You can't keep me locked up. I

haven't done anything wrong. Why don't you let me go? I won't tell anyone.'

The guard laughs again. 'You joking?' he says. 'Now just sit quietly till he comes.'

He clangs the door shut and Nona hears him turn the lock. She thinks over what the guard has said. She has never told a joke in her life.

She clings to the bars and watches him walk away, a huge bunch of keys dangling by his side.

'Let me out!' she shouts at him but he has rounded a corner and disappears from sight. She stands by the bars and sobs, then falls down onto her hands and knees and crawls into a corner.

This time she hears Bolverk before she sees him, his leather coat creaking as he approaches her cell. He doesn't come in but stands, sucking a sweet, watching her through the bars.

'Hasn't the guard told you that I didn't do it? I've told him. Why would I want to kill Thomas? I loved him.' She gets up and walks over to the door.

A new tear starts to roll down her cheek and

she quickly wipes it away. She doesn't want pity. Pitiful animals don't usually survive.

'Your prints were all over the gun. We like to make things tidy round here. Someone has to take the blame. An eye for an eye, as they say!'

'Well, what will happen to me?'

'You'll stand trial. Then you'll be convicted.'

'Then what?'

'Then you'll end up behind bars for the rest of your life.'

Nona's heart has not stopped beating fast since she was captured but now it seems to change gear and throb even faster. She tells herself not to show her weakness. That there'll be a way. Her hand goes down to her pocket to feel for the security of her knife. Sometime she'll be able to use it.

But it's not there.

'Looking for this?' Bolverk waggles the knife at her through the bars. 'Do you think we'd leave it on you?'

Nona stares at him, wondering how she hadn't noticed it go.

'My guards were all thieves and pickpockets at

one time. You're lucky you still have your shoes.'

Nona stares absently down at her feet.

'How long till this – trial?' she asks.

'Two weeks.'

'*Two weeks!* What am I supposed to do in here for two weeks?'

'Contemplate your wickedness.'

'*But I haven't done anything.* I keep telling you.' She clutches at the bars. 'I HAVEN'T DONE ANYTHING!'

'Enough of that! Now tell me your name.'

Now she has a name, Nona is afraid he'll take it away from her, and so she doesn't answer.

'I said – what's your name?' he hisses like a snake in a snake pit. It scares her.

'Nona.'

'Nona what?'

'Just Nona. Should I have another name?'

Bolverk takes a pair of leather gloves out of his pocket and puts them on. She notices his fat, pale fingers, which look like maggots.

'Not Bailey? Didn't he give you *his* name?'

Nona frowns and glares at him. She wants to

tell him he didn't even give her a first name but she can't bear the thought of this cruel man knowing things about her.

'It doesn't matter,' he goes on. 'No one will remember you. Now look straight at me and say your name and what you did. The judge will think more kindly of you if you admit to your crime.'

'My name is Nona. And I did *not* kill Thomas Bailey.'

'Thank you, Nona,' says Bolverk as he turns away. 'That will do very nicely. Oh – and, Nona . . .' he turns back for a moment. 'We have a little treat for you coming up.'

Nona goes back to her corner, wondering what treat could possibly be in store for her. She listens to his coat creaking down the corridor. She knows that he will play back the film of her arrest with great pleasure. Maybe pausing and replaying her moment of capture. The hand slipping into her pocket and taking the knife. Her tears. But she cannot know that he will edit her confession and remove the word *not* from her lips.

Chapter 17

Three days later she has a visitor.

Caius appears at the bars with one of the guards.

'Hello, Nona,' he says in a quiet voice.

'Caius!'

The guard walks away. 'You've got five minutes,' he says over his shoulder.

'What are you doing here?' says Nona.

'They know that my mother tried to turn you in. I just said I wanted to see you for myself so that I could report back.'

'Is that true?'

Caius rolls his eyes to the ceiling. '*No!* Of course not. What sort of person do you think I am?'

She smiles weakly at him. 'I don't seem to know anything any more. How's Jay?'

Caius scowls. 'He's fine. Look. I've got a plan. Well, it was Jay's plan. What time do they change the guard? Do you know?'

Nona thinks. 'The night guard comes on about seven p.m., then they change again in the morning around six a.m. They ring a bell at change-over.'

'Right. Be ready to leave tomorrow just before seven p.m. I'll be back. And, Nona . . .'

'What?'

'Just do what I say, OK? Don't ask *why*.'

The guard comes back down the corridor and taps Caius on the shoulder.

'Seen enough? Your five minutes are up.'

'Yes, thanks. My mother *will* be pleased.'

Nona spends the next day in great excitement. She paces up and down her cell, running her fingers along the bars. She even manages a smile when the guard comes round.

What had Jay and Caius in mind?

What was the plan?

She thinks about Jay and the bear and how pleased she'll be to see them again and she wonders if they're missing her.

Just before seven, Caius had said. At 6.30 she can hardly breathe with excitement. Then, to her dismay, she hears the creaking of Bolverk's coat as he approaches her cell.

'You still here?' He laughs.

Nona scowls at him. If this is a joke she's glad she's never told one. They seem cruel things.

He beckons to one of the guards, who approaches with a big bunch of keys.

'What's happening?' she asks as they undo the locks.

'You're going outside. Our little treat.' Bolverk takes her arm. 'There are some people who want to see you.'

The guard produces handcuffs and leg shackles from his pockets as if he were a magician taking a rabbit out of a hat.

'What are you doing?' Nona yells as he shackles

her ankles and clips the handcuffs to her wrists.

'Don't want you leaving us all of a sudden.' Bolverk nods with satisfaction.

Nona is furious, kicking out with her feet and pulling her hands, trying to free herself of the painful metal contraptions that hold her in place.

'Oh, there's just one last thing.'

Bolverk takes from his own pocket a collar, which he puts round Nona's neck then clips a lead to it and gives her a tug.

'I hear you were brought up by dogs?' He smirks. 'It's about time you were trained properly.'

They pull her down the corridor and out into the street. The bright lights cause her to flinch and she shuts her eyes as she is jerked and dragged towards the Circus. Every time she tries to stop, they yank her lead, causing her to choke as the collar tightens round her neck.

They pass the animals in their cages and stop next to the white lion, who barely lifts his head. The guard opens the door to the beast wagon next to him, unclips her lead and gives Nona a rough shove. With the manacles on her legs she can't find her balance and she falls onto the ground, rolling over into a tight ball. She hears the cage being locked and Bolverk's voice shout out to the gathering crowd.

'Come and see the next attraction! Come and see the Murderous Dog Girl.'

Nona stays where she has fallen, her head bent and her eyes shut tight.

She is aware of a mass of people staring at her through the bars. They want to see her face. They want to see her react. Someone slides a stick through the bars and pokes her. She thinks of the big bear she saw when she first arrived and wishes there was someone like her to snatch the stick away and tell them not to be so cruel.

After a while she lifts her head. People are standing outside her cage, pressing up to the bars. She sees Caius trying to push his way to the front. She wants to call out to him but stops herself. If he's caught trying to help her she'll never be able to escape. But she's thankful he's seen her. She was worrying that he would go to the prison and find her already gone.

Nona scrambles up and drags herself over to the bars.

Some of the people move back.

'Watch out! She might bite you!' someone says and a child in the front lets out a scream. Nona is tempted to bare her teeth and snarl at them – give them what they want – but she takes a deep breath and keeps her mouth shut.

Caius is now up to the bars himself and shoves a hand in to touch her.

'Watch out – she'll have that off!' a man next to him says. 'Apparently she ripped her guardian to pieces with her teeth!'

Caius turns on him.

'Oh, don't be so ridiculous. She did nothing of the sort. He shot himself. Took his own life. OK?'

The man pulls a face and shrugs.

Nona puts her face up to the bars and whispers to Caius, 'How am I going to get out now?'

He whispers back, 'They won't keep you here forever. I've still got that plan. Just hold on. Don't try anything stupid.'

Another man with a child on his shoulders

pushes Caius out of the way and Nona watches him being swallowed up by the sea of people.

She drags herself to the far corner of the cage and sits down with her back to them, refusing to play the part of the circus freak. On his first visit Bolverk had said her trial was in two weeks – that meant it was only ten days away now. Surely they wouldn't keep her in this cage for all that time? She begins to long for her old cell again. Anything, she thinks, would be better than this. Out of the corner of her eye she can see the white lion get up, stretch and begin to pace up and down. People leave her cage and watch him.

'That's right,' she says to herself. 'If I do nothing they'll go away.'

She wishes she had been put next to Mimi's cage, then at least she would be able to see Jay, but although she occasionally turns round and scans the crowd, he does not appear. Crow is a regular visitor though. He waggles his finger at her through the bars.

'See – I knew all along there was something about you,' he says. The monkey screams at her and climbs up the bars to the top, where he jumps up and down and waves his finger too.

She stays in the cage for two days. The guards shove food and water into her in bowls, expecting her to lap it up like a dog. But she refuses. Kids come and bark at her through the bars, but she remains defiant. She *will* get out and she *will* get to The Edge, she tells herself over and over again.

On the third day Bolverk appears with the guards.

'Just thought I'd let you know we've brought the date of your trial forward,' he says, clipping the lead to the collar that is still round her neck.

'When? When is it?'

'Tomorrow.'

Her mouth dries up and her heart is beating fast again. Perhaps he is taking her away now and she won't ever see Caius or the bear or Jay again. She'll never know what their plan was.

They lead her back to her old cell and Nona can see Bolverk scanning it for anything that might be out of order. There is still just a bed in there, a pillow, two blankets and a bucket. What on earth could she have done with them?

'So, enjoy your last night in this luxurious cell,' says Bolverk.

'W-what do you mean?' She is wondering if this is another joke. Though compared to being in the cage, this does seem like luxury. Of a sort.

'Oh, your next cell won't be nearly as nice as this. It's what you would call a *hell hole*.' He chuckles.

'You call this nice? There's nothing in it! This is crazy. I keep telling you I haven't done anything wrong.'

Nona is beginning to understand what crazy is and she knows for certain that compared to this, Jay is *not* and never has been – crazy.

Giving up hope that Caius might return she picks her bucket up and hurls it at the bars. It splits in two. Bolverk laughs, knowing that this will make good viewing later. Then she flings the pillow at him, and the blankets, and screams at the top of her voice.

Bolverk stops smiling. 'If you don't stop that noise I'll put you in the hole now. And believe you me – *that* is no luxury.'

'I hate you,' she shouts at him.

Turning sharply on his heel he marches off down the corridor.

'I hate you,' she says again, under her breath.

Nona paces up and down and then goes back to her bed. She has to get out. But how? She has no idea of the time now and no idea if Caius will ever return to carry out his plan. He doesn't know that her trial is the next day. Perhaps he'll come too late.

The time drags by, and now, without any company at all, she is feeling more and more desperate.

She hears the guard. 'You back? Who's this old lady?'

Caius's voice replies, 'This is my mother. She's not well, but she really wanted to see the girl before she goes down, and she arrived too late to see the spectacle outside.' Then he lowers his voice.

'*My mother is dying*. This is her last wish, you know.'

The guard grunts something then leads them to Nona's cell.

She sits on the bed and, after her initial excitement at hearing his voice, wonders why on earth Caius has brought his mother. It must have been a trick after all. Perhaps it had been Caius who told Bolverk where she was hiding all along. He hadn't come to Dissville to find her – he'd come for the reward money and to capture her. He'd told Bolverk that she hadn't burnt on the power lines. Perhaps they'd *all* told him.

Jay too.

But when she thinks of Jay she has a warm feeling in her stomach and she knows he would not betray her.

As they come into view she sees that the woman Caius is holding up is not his mother but Esmerelda, who is wearing the very long overcoat that Nona had seen her in when she first arrived at the circus. He has his arm round her waist like a ventriloquist's dummy, holding her above the ground at the height of his hip. Nona's mouth drops open in surprise.

The guard lets them in. 'You can go in her cell – she looks as if she's calmed down now. But only for five minutes – OK?'

When the guard is out of earshot Caius gently puts Esmerelda down and she stands, drowning in the overcoat, looking hardly bigger than a doll.

'Quick!' he says. 'Make a shape on your bed with that bucket – er, that *broken* bucket – and the pillow and cover it with a blanket. Make it look as if you're sleeping. When the guards change we can leave. The new guard will assume it is you in the bed.'

'But how am *I* supposed to leave?' asks Nona, looking at Esmerelda, who has a big grin on her face.

'Like when I do my act,' Esmerelda replies in her high-pitched voice. 'Only I'll be on *your* shoulders and wearing the overcoat. I'll just look normal size!'

They hear the bell ringing for the change-over.

'If they catch us you'll both end up behind bars too,' says Nona. 'I don't want you to risk this just for me.'

'Hey, Nona! Don't even think it. We're all going to The Edge, remember?' says Caius.

'And you too, Esmerelda?'

Esmerelda shakes her head. 'No. I'd be too frightened. I'm fine where I belong.'

Nona tries to make a figure under the blanket but to her it still looks like two halves of a bucket and a pillow.

'Here,' says Caius, 'let me do it. I'm an expert at this. I was always doing it at home when I was a small kid so that I could go out hunting for rats when I wasn't allowed to.'

In moments he has made a shape that looks just like a sleeping person. Then he gets Nona to bend down for Esmerelda to climb onto her shoulders and puts the long overcoat over them both. He nods with satisfaction. The new guard will not notice that Esmerelda is a good deal taller than when she arrived.

'We'll be out of here soon,' Caius whispers.

'Five minutes is up!' shouts the new guard as he jangles his way towards Nona's cell.

'Well, that was a waste of time!' says Caius, pushing his way past the guard. 'She went to bed and wouldn't talk to us. Either that or she's fallen asleep. Still, we've seen her and that's all we wanted.'

The guard peers over at Nona's bed.

'I'll wake her up for you,' he says, entering the cell. 'Hey, you in there. Get up and show some manners!'

'No!' says Caius a little too hurriedly, grabbing him by the arm. 'I mean, if you wake her she'll only start a fight with my mother – and my mother . . .' he lowers his voice again, 'is *dying*, you know.'

Outside, the pollution cloud has lowered and there is a thick mist swirling around the brightly lit streets. Visibility is low. When they are out of sight of the jail Nona drops down and Esmerelda slides to the ground.

'We must hurry. Jay is up on the hill with Mimi and the bear. Heaven knows how long we've got before they discover you've gone. We must put some distance between us and Dissville before they try and track us down,' says Caius.

'Those helicopters. They'll find us in no time.

Five of us, out in the open.' She pauses. Caius is grinning. 'Why are you looking like that, Caius?'

'I've put sugar in their petrol tanks.'

'What does that mean?'

'They won't be able to fly!'

Up on the hill wait Jay, Mimi and the bear.

When the bear sees her he rolls over and over, scrambling to his feet then running round in circles, waving his head from side to side.

'Wah! Wah!'

Nona hugs him and topples over, lost in the brown fur of his belly.

Mimi snarls at them both.

To Nona, Jay seems even taller than before, as if he's filled out, become someone – or something – else: stronger, more supple, more at ease in his skin.

He grins when he sees her, and Mimi snarls again.

Nothing is said. What must happen now is like a silent understanding.

With Jay followed by Caius leading the way, they head off towards The Edge.

Chapter 18

Away from the heat of the lights, the air is cold. Jay has brought Nona's fur-lined coat and he wraps it close to her body.

'I'm so tired,' she says. 'I didn't get any sleep in that horrible prison, or in the cage.'

'We can't stop – they'll be after us soon. We have to get going,' says Caius, looking over his shoulder.

Nona nods. 'Look at Mimi. She really doesn't like me, does she? She's making sure I keep my distance from you all right.'

They all stare at the big cat, who prowls around

them, her muscles tense beneath her fur.

'Just think about where we're going,' says Jay. 'It'll all be different. Just you see.'

She thinks of the wall and wonders how they'll get over it. She thinks of the snakes and shudders. She feels her eyelids drooping. She remembers Thomas Bailey teaching her to read with the aid of his ancient Natural History books, and names the snakes in her mind. King snakes, garter snakes, lyre snakes and red-tailed racers. Copperheads and cobras, coach whips, temple pit vipers and black-headed death adders.

The further they travel from Dissville the darker it becomes. Caius has a torch with him and shines it in front of them.

'Turn that thing off!' hisses Jay. 'Are you stupid or something? If someone was behind us they'd be able to see that beam. We don't need more light. We're fine.'

They trudge on in silence, all deep in their thoughts of the Green Wall and how and if they'll get there. Above them shines a blood-red moon. Nona thinks Jay is on edge and it makes her nervous.

'I'm sure we're being followed,' she says.

'Why do you think that?' says Caius. 'I can't hear anything.'

'I don't know. It's just a feeling.'

'What do you think, Jay?' Caius asks, trying to get back into Jay's good books.

Jay turns, his yellow eyes gleaming in the dark.

'I think Nona's right. But whatever it is it's a long way back. We must press on. How far do you think it is?'

Caius pulls a face, which in the dark only Jay can see.

'Dunno. Still a hell of a way I think.'

'What did you say the wall was like?' says Nona.

'Oh, I dunno. It's stupid, but to be honest I didn't really look too hard. I knew I shouldn't be there and when I saw the snake pit I just backed off and ran home. Well, I obviously didn't run *all* the way home. I'd been gone for several days.'

'I thought you said you were out looking for rats?' says Nona.

Caius turns bright red. 'Er – well, I was – sort of. But it was my stepfather really. I was trying to get away from him. I thought I'd be able to manage on my own but seeing that wall kinda scared me.'

'More scary than your stepdad? I bet he beat you even harder when you got back,' says Jay.

Caius nods.

'So how many snakes were there?' Nona asks.

'I don't know that either. I didn't actually *see* them.'

'Oh, great! There could be thousands of them and we'll never cross over.'

They continue their journey, Nona turning around every now and then, convinced that they are being closely followed. Jay won't let them stop till night turns to day and even then does not sleep himself. He prowls around, scanning the horizon behind them. He knows he should be grateful that Caius was able to disable the helicopters but he is cross about the way Nona looked at Caius in admiration and he is restless in the knowledge that their tracks are very easy to follow. Time was all they had on their side and he doesn't want to let it slip by.

'That's enough!' he shakes them by the shoulders when he sees that Nona and Caius have fallen asleep since they decided to stop. 'We'll have to keep going. They'll be on us if not.'

'But we've had no sleep!' Nona moans as she reluctantly clambers to her feet.

'Look – it was *you* that wanted to go to The Edge,' snaps Jay.

'I thought you wanted to go too,' Nona retorts.

They squabble as they set off again, then fall into silence until the day darkens and another night falls.

They all hear the noise at the same time and freeze, rooted to the spot.

As something moves towards them Mimi starts to growl.

'What's there?' Nona whispers to Caius.

Whatever it is springs out of the dark and knocks Caius to the ground. He cries out in pain and Mimi, standing her ground, her shoulder muscles quivering, lets out a warning roar. Another pair of eyes gleam in the night and Nona's hand has her arrow out of her pack in a flash and positioned in the bow. But she can't see what it is and wishes Caius had kept his torch on. She swings her bow towards the noise, though before she can let it off something has landed on her back, sending her flying.

Caius gets to his feet and, ignoring Jay's warning, takes the torch from his coat pocket. He switches it on and a huge grey wolf turns towards the light, its mouth curling back in a snarl, its paw placed firmly on Nona's back. For a split second, Nona thinks a look of disappointment passes over Caius's face.

Jay motions for her to be still but she already knows not to move. She shuts her eyes for a moment and waits for something to happen. Mimi is circling them and Nona imagines they'll both make a meal of her. Nona starts to make a low growling noise in her throat like the wolf and Caius shines the torch in its eyes, which disorientates it for a moment. Then Jay pulls his coat off and, with a huge leap, lands on the wolf, rolling it off Nona and pushing its jaws away. Nona jumps to her feet, shouting:

'Don't kill it, Jay! Please don't kill it.'

Jay looks up at her, his eyes shining, an expression on his face she has not seen before, his mouth open as if he is about to rip into the wolf with his own teeth.

'I said don't kill it, Jay.'

Jay shakes his head to hear her words, which to him sound as if they are coming from a long way away.

He lets go of the wolf.

The wolf springs to its feet and cowers back.

'It's one of your father's wolves,' says Nona in a shaky voice, turning to Jay, who is now patting Caius on the shoulder as if nothing out of the ordinary has happened.

'They said they didn't know how many wolves there were. I think it's – oh, I can't remember its name! I'm not sure which one it is – there were so many of them.'

'Well, I think that's all for the better,' says Jay. 'It doesn't need a name.'

'But I've got a name,' says Nona.

'That's different. *You're* not a wild animal.'

They all look towards the wolf.

'Poor thing,' says Nona. 'I feel sorry for it after all. It must be lonely. The only one left.'

'I guess there are other wolves in The Edge. That's why it's made its way here. It can sense them,' says Jay.

'It's hungry too, I think.' Caius takes a few steps back.

'That's an understatement!' says Jay.

Jay pulls some stale bread out of his pack and some strips of dried, processed meat.

'Are we all agreed the wolf should have it?'

Even though they are hungry themselves, Nona and Caius nod and watch Jay bend down and hold out the food to the starving wolf.

'Did you see Jay's face?' Caius whispers to Nona. 'Like he was possessed or something.'

She nods. 'But he saved me from being eaten.'

'Yeah, but I get a weird feeling off him. Like he's not exactly *normal*.'

The wolf starts to whine and falls down onto its stomach, edging its way across the ground to the outstretched hand.

'Hey, Caius, turn off that torch now. It'll be fine,' says Jay.

'Have you seen the bear?' asks Nona.

'He's moved on – I guess he doesn't need to be with us right now,' Jay answers.

Nona feels her spirits drop and she pulls her coat tighter around her.

When the dawn comes up they are able to take in their surroundings.

They are walking in a bleak landscape drawn by the wind. Here, away from Thomas Bailey's preserved piece of forest, nothing moves but the grass. There are no birds; no sign of carrion, as there is nothing to eat. No weasel or hare.

Nowhere to hide.

Without the choppers Jay reckons that if their pursuers pick up their trail, they'll be using vehicles and the dogs.

'We must keep going,' he says.

'I'm thirsty,' says Nona. 'My throat's feeling raw.'

'Yes,' moans Caius. 'Me too. Is there any water

left, Jay? Or something to eat?'

Jay stares at him, a look of contempt on his face. 'You're pathetic!' he says.

'We're not as strong as you are,' announces Nona, feeling sorry for Caius.

She says that to make Caius feel better but when she looks at Jay, he *does* seem stronger. She sees muscles on his arms and chest that she hasn't noticed before.

Jay ignores them and takes out the rest of the bread and the few slivers of dried meat. When they smell it Mimi and the wolf start growling again, circling them with hungry paces until Jay throws it towards them and lets them eat the remains.

'Oh, but I'm so starving too!' wails Nona.

'Look – if we don't feed them you know they would turn on us now,' says Jay.

'Mimi wouldn't do that to you though, would she?'

'Who knows? She's not in captivity any more – she can hear the call of the wild.'

'And you?' she says, thinking of the look on Jay's face. 'Can *you* hear the call of the wild?'

He gazes over the landscape and doesn't answer her.

Nona persists. 'What is it? What is the call of the wild? What's it like?'

Jay looks at her for a moment and she gets the feeling he has already crossed over to the other side.

'*I'll tell you about it one day*,' he says. 'See those mountains over there? That's where The Edge is! On the other side. Would you say so, Caius?'

'Yes,' says Caius. 'I think you could be right.'

Nona's lips feel dry and cracked; she doesn't care what Jay thinks of her and she is missing the bear. She offers some water to Caius from a bottle Jay hands her, then drinks the last few drops herself and wipes her mouth.

'Do you think they'd really bother to try and find us?' she asks Jay. 'Surely we're not worth it?'

'Bolverk's not a man to give up,' says Jay. 'He's set his heart on putting you away, whether or not you really killed my father. And besides . . .'

He stops and looks behind them. 'If we actually do make it, he won't want other people to try to get there too. He controls them all, see?'

Caius nods. 'Do you reckon we'll make it?'

Nona stares at him and thinks he seems changed too. His face, the only part of him she can see, looks pale and grey and his eyes have lost their shine.

'Are you OK?' she asks.

He nods again but when Jay strides on ahead he whispers in Nona's ear. 'I'm scared. I know I shouldn't say that but I am.'

'What are you scared of, Caius?'

'That tiger for a start! Have you noticed how fierce she's looking? She's not Jay's little pet any more. And that wolf and – well – Jay. *He* scared me for a moment.'

She nods and they carry on walking, their heads bent, gazing at the ground as they go. It is because of this that they hear them before they see them. There is a loud flapping noise above their heads and the sky seems to darken, as if something has blotted out the sun. There is a terrible smell, like rotting meat, and, when the screaming comes, Caius, Nona and Jay jerk their heads up in horror.

'Oh my God!' whispers Nona. 'What on earth are *they*?'

Above their heads circle a pair of monstrous black birds with a wingspan of several metres. They have ragged feathers and Nona can see they have talons on them like daggers. She has never seen birds like it.

'Scags,' says Jay, grimly. 'They've sent the scags.'

Chapter 19

The birds continue to fly over their heads, flapping their wings and causing dust to billow up in clouds.

'Scags? What sort of birds are they?' Nona says, holding her nose to block out the awful stench.

'They're not real birds,' says Jay. 'I never thought they'd send *them* out.'

'But what are they doing?'

'They're spying on us.'

'What do you mean?' says Caius. 'How can they do that? Are they going to fly back and tell Bolverk where we are?'

'Yes. Sort of.'

'You're not telling us they can *speak*, are you?' Caius steps back, not taking his eyes off the birds in case they attack him.

Jay shakes his head. 'Look at their eyes. Do they look weird to you?'

'They look *altogether* weird,' says Nona. 'Did your father have a hand in these too?'

'I don't know,' says Jay. 'It's possible, I suppose.'

'Yeah,' says Caius, peering at them closely. 'They're like mirrors. And much too big for their heads.' He pauses for a moment then lets out a yelp. 'They're like Bolverk, aren't they? Those aren't eyes – they're *cameras*!'

They watch as the birds continue to swoop above their heads, diving towards them then soaring up in the sky again.

'So they know exactly which direction we've gone in,' says Nona. 'Oh, I can't bear it! That horrible man will take their eyes out, plug them into his computer and watch everything we do.'

'Not if we can stop them,' says Jay.

'But how? We can't reach them.'

'You'll have to shoot them. And you'll have to be quick, they've probably seen enough.'

'How do they know when they've seen enough? Have they got a mind?'

'No! They're not that clever. Bolverk will have them on some sort of remote control.'

'Well, how will *he* know?'

'Oh, Nona – stop asking questions! Just get on and do it!' Jay shakes his head then takes in a deep breath. 'Oh, God. I know now. They're filming us *live*!'

'You mean he's watching us now?'

'Yeah! I'm certain he is. Quick. You need to shoot them!'

Nona slips her pack off and, with shaking hands, she removes her bow from the bag.

'Turn your back,' says Caius. 'Don't let them see what you're doing. Bolverk'll call them back if he knows you're going to shoot them.'

She reaches inside for some arrows, quickly positions one in her bow, then spins round and takes aim. For a moment the birds seem to trick her, make her believe that they are real, that they are the first living, truly wild creatures they've come across on their journey to The Edge. She hesitates.

'Go on!' yells Jay. 'For God's sake, Nona, shoot!'

She jolts back into reality and lets the arrow fly. It catches one of the birds square on its chest and, with a scream, it plummets to the ground.

'Oh! Are you sure it's not real?' she cries. 'I've killed it.'

'Quick! Quick! Get the other one before it goes!' yells Jay. 'I keep telling you they're not real.'

But Nona's next arrow is caught in her pack and she loses valuable seconds before she can position it in the bow. With a screech the other scag dives towards her, its dagger-like talons stretched out in front of it. She lets the arrow fly but the bird is approaching so fast she can't aim properly and the arrow shoots wide of its mark. The noise and the smell of the bird which is now almost on top of her causes Nona to shrink back and, just as the creature is about to land on her and rip her eyes out, Jay springs forward like a huge cat, hitting the bird away with his fist and covering Nona with his body. The bird shrieks and flies vertically up into the sky and before Nona can recover and place another arrow in her bow – it has gone.

'Damn!' curses Jay. 'Now Bolverk will know exactly where to find us and send the men out.'

He walks over to the other scag, which is lying, jerking, on the ground, its wings smashed. Jay picks its head up and shouts at its one remaining eye.

'You won't get us, Bolverk! We'll get there and you won't be able to stop us!'

Then he stamps on the bird's head, smashing the camera into tiny pieces and scattering shards of metal and glass across the ground.

'That was stupid,' Caius whispers to Nona as Jay picks the remains of the scag up and hurls it into the distance. 'That's going to provoke Bolverk even more. Jay's got really unpredictable lately. I don't know that I can trust him.'

The grey sky overhead threatens another bout of snow and already a few flakes are drifting down. Nona's heart is still pumping fast from the scag attack but the rush of adrenalin makes her forget her tiredness and she strides out after Jay. Occasionally she catches sight of the bear sniffing the ground ahead of them and seeing him lifts her spirits and puts a lightness into her step. They carry on walking for the next few hours.

The snow is heavy now and beginning to lie thickly on the ground. It starts to slow them down and walking is harder. Nona crams a handful of snow into her mouth to take away her thirst. It is so cold now that she has to pull the sleeves of her coat over her hands to keep her fingers warm. She opens and clenches her fists, trying to get the circulation going, and she notices that Caius is doing the same thing.

'Aren't you cold, Jay?' she calls out, but Jay either does not hear or chooses to ignore her. He is pacing ahead with no sign of coldness in his body.

'I crossed a river,' Caius suddenly announces after they've been walking for a few more miles. 'We should come across it soon, I guess, though we're not in exactly the same place that I was. It was quite wide in parts and it took ages to find a place I could cross.'

Nona immediately thinks of all that water she could drink to ease her parched throat. Then she remembers how, when she first escaped from Thomas Bailey's farm, she and the bear had swum across a river to escape the men and their dogs. *That damned river.* She doesn't relish the thought of doing it again. She shakes her head. *That damned river.* What is happening to her? She seems to be getting less confident the nearer to The Edge she gets. Perhaps Caius's fears are rubbing off on her. Certainly it is having the opposite effect on Jay.

They are walking across a vast moor, frozen underfoot.

Nona grabs hold of Caius's arm and shuts her eyes, letting her feet stumble along at his side, her thoughts on the water she'll soon be able to drink. She hears Mimi's growling coming from somewhere behind them but is too weary to watch her back.

'Can you hear that noise? Is it Mimi?'

They stop. Caius can hear nothing. But it is not the tiger behind them.

Jay turns around. He lifts his head and puts his finger to his lips.

'Engines. That's the sound of a truck. They've found our trail. Come on!'

Nona is now wide awake again, mouth-filling fear pumping through her body. She finds the strength to run and, letting go of Caius's arm, the three of them take off across the moor, leaving a trail of footprints in the snow. The ground is rising steeply and travelling is hard work.

'We're nearly there, right?' Nona says under her breath to Caius, who is now breathing heavily. She resists the temptation to turn around to see where their pursuers are.

'I don't know. Like I said. We're not in the same place. But I guess that wall runs for miles. We must be close.'

'I thought you said you knew! We could be going in the wrong direction. We could be going *anywhere*. What's going to happen to us? We haven't even crossed the river.'

Nona grasps her coat to her body and wonders if she was wrong to have had such faith in him.

Now even Caius can hear the truck. They turn and look behind them.

'Oh my God!' says Caius. 'What on earth is that thing?'

A huge black vehicle is bouncing over the rocks and boulders towards them, nothing seeming to get in its way. The bear, the wolf and the tiger are further ahead, a dusting of snowflakes settling on their fur, unaware of the strange beast that is fast approaching them.

Chapter 20

Jay is now sprinting over the ground as if he were on fire. For a moment Nona forgets what they are running from and watches in awe at his speed. When he reaches the horizon she can see him stop and wave as if beckoning them to come quickly. Caius and Nona start to run, following the tracks of the bear, the tiger and the wolf. Jay's footprints are not to be seen; his feet have barely made any impact on the hard snow.

When they reach him he grins at them.

'Look! The river's down there!'

Nona looks down the sweep of the land and,

beneath them, lies a vast river.

'It's frozen!' she says. For a moment she thinks of how thirsty she is. Then – 'Thank goodness we won't have to swim it!'

'But that's not good,' says Caius, panting as he approaches them. 'That monster behind us will be able to cross it too. It would have been better if the river had been flowing – like it should be. It's crazy to find a big river frozen like that.'

They look down to where the river, caught in a moment of time, would have swept round the bend on its way to the sea. The bear and the tiger are sniffing around its shores, the wolf already trotting on its frozen surface.

'Come on – we've got to get a move on. That truck is gaining on us.' Jay pulls Nona's sleeve.

'But where are we running to? There's no shelter anywhere,' she cries.

'Round that bend, following the river. There'll be something there, I'm sure. Caius, do you recognise where we are?'

Caius shakes his head, his eyes downcast. He had wanted to lead them to freedom.

They take off once more, tearing down the slope and reaching the banks of the river as the black truck appears on top of the hill. Nona puts a foot on the ice and her feet give way from under her and she slips, landing hard.

'Here,' says Caius, pulling at the reeds that stand stiffly by the shoreline. 'Strap these under your boots. You'll get a better grip.'

He takes a knife from his pocket and cuts lengths off the end of the string which holds up his trousers, then helps tie the reeds to the bottom of Nona's boots. He offers some to Jay, but Jay shakes his head.

'I'm fine,' he says. 'But hurry!'

When Caius has done the same to his own boots they start to cross. The reeds grip the ice and they are able to slip and slide without falling over. The sun comes out and the ice turns a silvery blue. In spite of the dreadful black truck getting closer, Nona can see that this is a place of great beauty. They have to be nearing The Edge. Here, Nature, not Bolverk, is beginning to take control.

'Do you think the ice is safe?' she asks, keeping

an eye on the bear, who has found a hole in it and is trying to catch a fish with his paw.

'It'll have to be,' says Jay. 'We're not as heavy as the bear. Keep away from his hole and watch where the others go.'

They are halfway across when they feel the ice start to thrum and vibrate. They turn round and see that the truck is crossing the river after them. As it draws nearer they can see the true size of it – built like a tank with blacked-out windows and riding on enormous wheels. They dread how many people it must contain, people who could leap out of the doors at any moment with their guns and stop them.

The bear has abandoned his hole and is nearly on the other side. Nona does a double take. The bear has started to *swim*.

'Oh my God!' she cries out. 'The ice is melting!'

She looks down at her feet and sees the river water moving rapidly under the ice. They hear a loud cracking noise and a deep fissure opens up.

The truck is closing in on them and they stand, rooted to the spot, wondering which is the safest way to go. Suddenly the truck's back end drops and a huge section of the ice gives way. With a strange sucking noise, the vehicle disappears into the water, leaving a yawning hole in the ice.

They stand there, looking at where the truck had been, for ages, wondering if anyone will climb back out of the hole. But it is silent, and each one of them imagines what has happened to the man or men inside. When it is clear that no one is climbing out, Caius wants to go over but Jay won't let him.

'The ice'll be too thin. Come on, we've got to get off it ourselves.'

Another crack zigzags across the surface. He takes Nona's hand and pulls her along after him.

'Look – the animals are over. We'll be OK. We just need to get off this surface before it gives way.'

As they near the other side, the ice has melted completely and the water is flowing fast and furious round the bend in the river. Jay lets go of Nona's hand and leaps onto the bank. She looks back at Caius and knows they are both thinking the same thing.

How could anyone human leap across such a wide space?

Nona pauses to get her breath, letting the warm sunlight play on her face.

She watches as Caius tries to copy Jay. He runs and takes off but he can only make half the distance that Jay had and falls into the water. He cries out and disappears.

'Do something, Jay! Help him,' Nona shouts but Jay just stands on the bank, staring. Within seconds Caius's head bobs up again further along the river and he splashes out for the shore. Relief sweeps over her and she watches Jay lean across and offer his hand. He drags Caius out of the water and lays him on the bank.

'Come on, Nona!' Jay yells at her. 'It's all melting!'

She starts to tread lightly towards them, knowing she'll have to swim the last bit, but another crack rings out and, before she can get off, the ice opens up and sucks her in.

Nona is a good swimmer but the current is too strong for her and it whisks her away, pulling her under the surface of the ice. She fights for air as she is dragged down and tries to hit the ice over her head with her fist. She can see the rays of sun through the surface, can hear the rushing of the current at her side and begins to swallow water as her breath runs out. She had yearned for a drink – but not like this. Suddenly she is flung up to the surface, the ice breaking up around her ears. She gasps and splutters but, now her head's out of the water, she can hear its fatal roaring as it sweeps her towards the bend of the river. With a sickening feeling she knows what lies beyond. The water is spraying up against the rocks with a huge force. The wild current is taking her, surely, towards a waterfall, which will be impossible to survive.

Nona does not have enough breath to call out but she knows the boys have seen what is happening. The current tosses her up against the rocks and she tries to grab hold of them as she rushes past.

'Nona!' she hears someone shout above the noise of the rushing water, and sees Jay tearing along the riverbank. As she goes under she thinks how amazing Jay looks, running and leaping over the rocks like a stag.

Her head comes up again and she manages to grab another breath of air as she sees him dive into the water at the point where the river sweeps round the bend to the waterfall. She can feel herself being pulled along so fast now that her limbs seem to have nothing to do with her. She is spun round and round as she nears the edge of the fall.

Strong arms grab her round the waist and she kicks out in fear.

'Be still, Nona!'

She hears a voice above the roar of the water but her instinct is to struggle and push Jay down so she can keep her head above the surface of the river. Now she can see where the water is cascading over the edge and she gives up fighting. Her body relaxes and Jay's arm stays round her. He grabs hold of a rock with his other arm and pulls them back from the top of the waterfall. The force is so great that his face contorts in pain but he hangs on. Releasing his arm from round Nona's waist he catches hold of her with his legs, which tighten around her body and keep her head above water. With his free hand he grabs another rock.

By this time Caius has scrambled over to them along the bank. He has the rope they'd bought in Dissville to scale the Green Wall and he shouts out to Jay, 'Catch it! I'll try and haul you in!'

He throws it into the tearing water but it falls short and he has to drag it back. On the third attempt, Jay is able to grab the end of the rope and pull them round the rock. But Caius isn't like Jay and he lacks the strength to hold on. He can feel the rope slipping through his fingers and he cries out, 'No! No! I can't . . .'

It is unusual for Caius to panic, but the thought of losing his friends, particularly Nona, jolts him back into action. He sees a tree stump jutting out nearby and, with the last bit of the rope, manages to wrap it round the trunk. It takes the pressure off and he holds on now, watching Jay pull himself and Nona clear of the treacherous water with superhuman strength.

Chapter 21

'Bolverk won't stop, you know,' says Jay as they lie on the rocks, letting the sun dry their bodies. 'I'm sure there are other people and vehicles on our trail.'

Caius looks up at the mountain ahead of them. 'We've got to get over that mountain,' he says. 'They'll have to come on foot. Even their vehicles won't get up that.'

'Will Bolverk follow us? If we get over the wall?' asks Nona.

Jay shakes his head.

'He needs to stop us before we do. The other side

of the wall is going to be a different world. Dad never talked about it – perhaps he was afraid I'd try and find it.' He stretches out. 'I don't think Bolverk would enjoy being in it. He may be Chief of Police here, but over there . . .' Jay tightens his lips, 'he'd lose his power. It's not somewhere he'd belong.'

'How do we know *we'd* belong?'

'We don't. But I know I don't belong in *Dissville*. I've seen The Edge in my dreams. It's a place I can find some sort of peace. If I hadn't met *you*, Nona, I'd still be in that miserable Circus.'

He looks at her. 'I think you set my dreams alight.'

She smiles at him. 'Is it really just on the other side of the mountain? The Edge?'

'It's close,' says Jay. 'Can't you feel it drawing you like a magnet?'

Nona is not sure that she can and turns towards Caius to see if he agrees. He is looking miserably at the ground.

Nona sits up and looks around.

'My pack! Where're my bow and arrows?'

'They're fine! They're over there. You strapped

203

them so close to your body not even that waterfall would have taken them from you,' says Jay, grinning at her.

She relaxes. 'I wish we'd set all the other animals free when we left,' Nona says. 'All those poor creatures, stuck behind bars for the rest of their lives.'

'Yeah – but it would have been impossible. Most of them are like those kids on reins – they wouldn't know where to go,' says Jay, idly tossing a small stone into the river.

'I did release one,' says Caius, looking up.

'You did what?' says Nona with a surprised look on her face.

'I set that white lion free. I couldn't bear to see it in that cage. It reminded me of me. My stepfather used a whip on me and sometimes he'd chain me up too. I couldn't stand thinking of it spending the rest of its life behind bars – whilst we . . .' He hesitates. 'Whilst we are *free*.'

Jay gets up and slaps him on the back.

'Well done, then! I don't know how you managed it – they keep them under lock and key.'

'I picked the lock,' Caius says.

Nona touches him on the arm and smiles at him and, for the first time, she sees him smile back.

'Where do you think it is?' she says.

Caius shrugs.

'I thought it might have been him when that wolf leapt out. Perhaps he's already there.'

They set off towards the mountain. They can still see the tracks of the bear, the wolf and the tiger in the snow, and they follow them. The animals seem to know the easiest route and they walk up the trail that they have made.

'We're not far now, are we?' Nona asks Caius. 'Do you think we could stop just for a moment?'

'It's not up to me. Ask Jay.'

But Jay is too far ahead to ask.

They round some rocks and notice the animals' prints have gone off in different directions.

'I wish the bear was here,' says Nona. 'I wonder if I'll see him again.'

'Well, I don't care if I don't set eyes on that tiger again! I hope we've seen the last of her,' says Caius.

But he has spoken too soon.

Some small rocks tumble down the slope above them and Caius and Nona look up to see what has caused them to fall, expecting to find Jay grinning at them. Instead they see Mimi. The tiger looks magnificent. Although she's clearly starving, her coat has acquired a gleam. She appears to dominate the whole landscape.

Caius and Nona stand still, watching, as Mimi slowly comes back down the path towards them.

Nona pulls her bow out of her pack, not taking her eyes off the tiger for a moment. Mimi stops, twisting her massive head, and snarls at them.

'Jay!' shouts Nona, bringing up her bow. 'It's Mimi!'

Jay turns round to see Mimi explode from the undergrowth and pound towards Nona and Caius.

Nona screams out.

'Stop her! I don't want to kill her!'

She has the arrow in position and the bow drawn back as Jay runs back towards them.

But the bear is there first, appearing from nowhere, standing on his back legs and flashing his claws like a set of knives. Mimi shrinks back and lashes out with her own claws. In seconds they are locked in a vicious, snapping, spitting embrace. Nona's hand is shaking again as she aims her arrow, terrified that she will hit the bear by mistake. Then Jay calls out to Mimi – a loud, inhuman noise that has Mimi roll over on her back and the bear drop down onto all fours.

Jay still has power over Mimi, Nona thinks, but not as the boy she once knew.

The bear lets Nona hug him and the warmth from his body gives her new strength. They continue the climb but they all keep well away from Jay and Mimi.

The mountain isn't high and it isn't long before they are slipping down the other side. Foothills lie in front of them, which are far easier to climb, and Nona begins to feel excited again. She can keep an eye out for the bear, grateful that he still feels protective towards her.

On the peak of the second hill Jay has stopped. He is silhouetted against the skyline. As he turns Nona can see his face light up. He waves at them.

'We're here!' he shouts. 'We're here!

Chapter 22

A green wall runs along the ridge of the next hill. From where they stand it looks huge, following the contours of the land as far as they can see.

'How are we going to get over that?' says Nona.

'We've still got that rope,' replies Jay. 'Once one of us is over we can pull the others up.'

'But we can't pull a wolf up or a tiger or a bear.'

'We'll find a way. We'll try and break through from the other side.'

'But what about the snakes? How are we going to cross those snakes?'

They stare at the wall, the vast pit in front of it and the wire fence built to hold back the snakes.

'We'll do it, Nona. We've come this far. Anyway, we can't turn back,' says Jay.

'I know. There's nowhere to run to!' She laughs, despite herself.

'Ssssh!' says Caius. 'Have you noticed that noise?'

'What noise?'

'Barking.'

'They'll be on foot now with the dogs. Come on – let's get to that wall,' urges Jay, rushing ahead to the snake pit.

Mimi and the bear are already there and the wolf is trying to dig under the wire through the settling snow. Nona holds her breath, willing herself to look over the edge at the heap of slithering, sliding snakes. She peers through the wire.

Jay is roaring with laughter.

'Snakes? What snakes? There aren't any!'

They all stare down into the pit and see the remains of a few half-eaten snakes and a mass of many more skeletons, their delicate shapes looking like the veins on a leaf, partly hidden under the snow.

'So people have been afraid of nothing!' says Nona, brushing white snowflakes away from her face.

'But they *were* there,' says Caius. 'Look! That's pretty frightening, isn't it?'

He points to something moving in the pit and Nona shudders. It's a two-headed snake, writhing and twisting and rolling over in the snow. She gasps. Those books on snakes never featured a snake with two heads, she thinks, until she realises what is happening.

'They've all eaten each other!' Nona says under her breath. 'Those are the last two. That snake – it's got the other one in its mouth.'

'Come on – we haven't got time to look at that. They're coming!' says Jay, and he and Caius begin to rip up the wire that once held back the mass of serpents that lived in the pit. The bear and the tiger and the wolf are already in there and running alongside the wall. Nona, watching them, marvelling how close they all are now, hears the sound of the pack of dogs coming up the hill. A volley of gunshot sends the bear, wolf and tiger tearing off along the pit. She peers through a thick flurry of snow to see where the bear is. He is there, standing on his hind legs and clawing at the wall until, suddenly, he is gone.

Nona tries to push herself under the wire but the hood of her coat gets snagged and she is stuck.

'Quick! Quick!' shouts Jay, running to her side and pulling up the wire. There is a ripping sound as Nona struggles free of her coat and falls into the pit.

'The bear's gone!' she wails. 'Where is he?'

'Where did you see him last?' Caius has now come to her aid and she points further along the wall. 'The tiger and the wolf have gone too.'

The guns go off again, louder, nearer than before.

'There must be a hole. A hole in the wall!' Nona cries out as she runs, slipping on snake corpses, towards the place where the bear disappeared.

What she sees, however, is not a hole. When she

touches the wall her hand goes straight through it. Instead of being made of thick, green stone – the wall is a hologram.

Caius opens his mouth in amazement.

'An illusion! The whole thing is an illusion to keep people in. I don't believe it! How stupid we all are!' His face crumples and he looks as if he is about to burst into tears.

Nona touches his arm.

'You weren't to know. People believe in fear. Your dad', she turns to Jay, 'always used to say there was nothing to fear but fear itself!'

But Jay is not listening. He is looking up to the top of the pit, where a man in a leather coat is pointing a gun.

'Pass through that wall. Hurry!' he says under his breath.

Caius dives through the hologram, holding out his hand to take Nona with him, but –

'Stop!' Bolverk shouts as he releases the safety catch on his gun and takes aim. 'I'll shoot you if you don't stop.'

Nona and Jay back slowly towards the wall.

Another step or two and they could just disappear through it. But Bolverk is joined by three or four other men, all with rifles pointed at them.

'You'll kill us anyway,' Nona shouts back. 'Once people know that this wall couldn't keep anyone in they'll all come here.'

'You are right! *They'll never know, if you can't tell them*,' shouts Bolverk.

And Bolverk's finger pulls the trigger and releases the bullet that flies towards her and before she can do anything, before she can get through the wall or turn away, Jay has stepped in front of her and the bullet enters his body.

Chapter 23

On the other side of the hologram the ground falls away steeply. Jay's body falls back onto Nona and they disappear through the wall and tumble down the other side. He lies at the bottom, a thin trickle of blood staining the snow. Caius rushes to Jay's side as Nona scrambles up and pulls away his clothing to get to the wound. Caius gasps as he sees the scars covering Jay's body.

'Oh my God! What happened to him?'

He looks up at Nona, who is taking no notice of him and has tears streaming down her face.

'I hate him! That Bolverk! I hate what he's

done to everyone. How he's ruined everything and now – Jay. He's killed him, hasn't he? I'm going back to stop him. I'll make sure he never does anything again.'

Nona grabs her bow and scrambles up the slope. She walks through the hologram in such a fury that she couldn't have cared less if Bolverk and his men had crossed the snake pit and were coming for her.

But they are still standing there on the other side.

'Bolverk!' Nona shouts, climbing to her feet, her bow poised, the arrow ready for its flight. 'What was it you said? *An eye for an eye?*'

He looks up. She sees him, in his greasy leather coat, a cruel smile on his face, his cyber-eye gleaming in the light.

She takes aim, draws back her arm and lets the arrow fly from the bow.

Before he has time to lift his gun the arrow hits his eye. She sees it explode with a flash of light and Bolverk fall to the ground.

'That's one piece of film you won't be able to

play,' she says under her breath as she throws herself back through the wall and slides down into The Edge.

Caius lies with his head on Jay's chest, holding up his hand to quieten Nona.

'He's still breathing,' he says. 'We've got to get that bullet out. Have you got a knife? I left mine by the river.'

Nona shakes her head. 'Are you sure?' she whispers. 'Sure he's still alive?'

Caius nods impatiently. 'Give me one of your arrows then.'

Nona takes an arrow from its sheath and snaps its end off, handing him the sharp tip. His hands are steady as he places it on Jay's chest.

'His breathing is really slow. The bullet has just missed his heart – he's lucky.'

He takes a handful of snow and wipes away the blood before cutting the tip into the wound and dislodging the bullet. He prises it up gently and dislodges it with his fingertips. Blood is now streaming from Jay's shoulder.

'We've got to stop all this bleeding,' says Caius,

pulling up his jacket and ripping a strip off his T-shirt. 'We'll pack the wound with snow. Then we'll tie this round the top part of his chest.'

They work quickly, wrapping his chest and shoulder tight with the cloth.

'All those scars. What happened to him?' Caius asks again. 'Was he attacked by something?'

Nona shrugs. 'Maybe. Maybe he was attacked by . . . a tiger. He's alive, though. That's the best thing.'

Jay opens his eyes and blinks.

'Where am I?' he asks.

'In The Edge! We're in The Edge. We made it!' says Nona, holding his hand. Jay's face screws up in pain.

'Where's the pochine?' Nona asks. 'It'll help.'

'I've left it behind. This is a different kind of pain.' He smiles weakly at her. 'It'll be fine. It really will.'

He tries to sit up and sees the blood in the snow. He puts his hand to his chest and then covers his ears.

'My God. What happened? I don't remember.

There's such a noise in my head.'

Caius and Nona look at each other and raise their eyebrows.

'You were shot by Bolverk,' says Caius.

Jay struggles to his feet.

'Oh, yes. I remember now. That wall – it wasn't real.'

He looks around and shakes his head. 'What *is* that noise?'

They shrug their shoulders, unable to hear anything but the thumping of their own hearts.

'I'm starving too, aren't you?' Jay says. 'Hey – the bear! What's happened to the bear?'

Nona looks around her in despair.

'Oh, no – he's gone! I forgot about him for a moment. I didn't see him go. He just went through that wall and . . . I didn't say goodbye!'

Jay puts an arm around her, then suddenly picks her up and spins her round, breaking into a crazy dance as he does so.

'But, Nona – it's what you wanted, isn't it? For him to be free and wild again? It's like he's grown wings!'

He is clasping her so tightly round the waist that Nona can't answer him, her hair still just long enough to fly around her and whip him in the face as he throws his head back and roars with laughter.

'Jay! JAY! Put her down. You've just been shot. Watch that wound.' Caius is shouting and trying to step in but Jay carries on, spinning her faster and faster.

'You've got wings too, Nona!'

There is a huge clap of thunder and Nona screams out. Jay drops her to the ground.

'It's what you wanted though, isn't it? For the bear? For him to be free and wild?' he says, as if nothing has happened.

Nona looks up at him in astonishment. Jay is scaring her.

'Yes.' She fights back her tears as she picks herself up. 'I know it's right, but I miss him.'

'You'll see him again. He's not going to forget you,' says Caius, helping her to her feet. But Jay has already forgotten Nona and is scanning the landscape as another clap thunders through the sky.

Caius turns up the collar on his coat and thrusts his hands into his pockets.

'What's with that crazy dancing?' he whispers to Nona.

As she shrugs, the sound of a gun goes off and a bullet whistles past them, landing in the snow. They all turn at once and see, standing on the top of the slope – the figure of Bolverk. His face is covered in blood, a hole where his cyber-eye had been. He staggers towards them, his gun aimed in their direction.

'You'll never be able to tell them!' he shouts. 'I won't let you!'

He shoots again but he can hardly see now. Nona, Jay and Caius begin to run, bullets flying randomly around them.

The sound of the gun has startled a flock of birds that launch themselves, squawking, into the sky. Then a huge shape leaps out from behind a rock, snarling and roaring as it pounds towards Bolverk.

'Mimi!' says Jay under his breath.

She is joined by the grey wolf, who seems to

appear from nowhere, and within seconds they are at the bottom of the slope. Mimi leaps first, landing on Bolverk's chest and knocking him to the ground, then the wolf, his jaws open wide, starts to pull at his leg.

Bolverk lets out a scream of terror as Nona, Jay and Caius look on helplessly, their mouths hanging open in horror.

The animals are still tearing at Bolverk when the brown shape of the bear joins them. Nona turns away, unable to watch.

'So, for Bolverk, at least,' she says, 'his fear of the wild was justified.'

'I'm going to get some food,' Jay says. 'I don't think I've ever been so hungry.'

Nona and Caius stare at him.

'I don't think I could eat anything after *that*,' says Caius.

'Come on – let's explore. We're here! There's nothing to stop us. We can do anything, go anywhere.' Jay lifts his head and sniffs the air. '*Come on!*' He quickens his pace and soon he is racing towards the forest.

Nona takes Caius's arm. 'I can hear stuff too,' she says. 'I think it's what Jay meant when he described it as the *call of the wild*. It's like you can hear stuff breathing.'

But Caius just looks at her blankly.

The huge expanse of forest lies in front of them. Jay nears the first of the trees. He stops and turns and waves an arm above his head, a big smile sweeping across his face.

'Do you think the forest is real or is it a hologram too?' Nona asks Caius.

He peers towards Jay, narrowing his eyes in the wind.

'Whatever it is he's gone into it,' he says. 'It's real, all right.'

Nona wrinkles up her nose. 'Yes. I can smell the trees too. Shall we go?'

She holds onto Caius's arm again and they follow Jay's footprints.

'I wish he'd waited for us,' she says.

'We'll find him,' says Caius.

Caius stops and wipes his brow, which is glistening with beads of sweat.

'It's not quite how I imagined it,' he says 'And this wind is rattling my bones and making me feel uneasy.'

He looks beyond the trees to where enormous, jagged peaks soar up into the clouds. Fierce, threatening rocks hold the remnants of bushes, twisted and gnarled like people hurrying across the landscape.

'This wilderness does what it likes, doesn't it? It seems restless.'

'Caius! I didn't know you could be so miserable. *You're* the one that seems restless.'

'Like I said before. Part of me is scared. I love the fact that life is all around us but it's dangerous here. If we got lost we could die.'

'I can't believe you don't hear that noise,' says Nona as they enter the forest. 'All life is on the go. Shifting, moving, creeping, jumping. You *must* be able to hear it!'

Caius stops.

'Ssssh,' he whispers.

'What?'

'Don't you feel as if someone's watching you?'

They stand still, their eyes darting around for a glimpse of other human life. There is a rustling noise behind them and they turn, moving closer together. A small deer leaps through the undergrowth, its eyes wide with fear. It stops for a moment when it sees them then takes off again at high speed. There is another crashing noise and a larger, more powerful creature, the colour of the snow, bursts through the undergrowth.

It is the white lion.

Caius gasps and it too stops for a moment, staring at them. Then, tossing back its head, it opens its jaws in a grinding snarl and follows the deer into the forest.

Nona glances at Caius and sees tears streaming down his face.

'He made it!' he whispers.

Chapter 24

Inside the forest everything is green. It glistens like a jewel. The snow has not penetrated the roof of the trees. It's as if The Edge can disguise itself in a hundred different costumes. Here in the trees it appears as sweet as honey, drinking the fine mist of moisture and sunlight that falls through the leaves.

'Nothing is what it seems,' says Caius, looking at a rotting leaf that turns out to be a moth.

Nona scratches her arm, which is covered in tiny, red itchy spots. 'Where is he? Where's Jay?'

What they cannot know is the transformation that

is taking place in the forest. Jay is becoming a thing of the wild, his shadow appearing and disappearing amongst other shadows. He prowls quietly through the trees, unnoticed amidst the dappled light.

'Let's go back,' says Caius.

'What? To Dissville?' says Nona.

'No! I'd *never* go back there. Let's go back into the open. I want to see more of what's out there.'

Caius leads them out of the forest. The snow has disappeared, all tracks melted into the ground.

'We mustn't lose Jay,' says Nona.

'He'll be fine,' says Caius. 'He's home now. He's not worried about us, is he? Come on.'

They walk together towards the mountains and now even Caius begins to hear the sounds around him. The rattles and squeaks.

Peque peque peque. Everything on the move.

They follow the trails made by animals, pushing their way through brambles and scrambling over fallen branches.

They reach a huge lake surrounded by rocks and caves. They hear the odd splash of creatures sliding and slipping back into the water. A pair of eyes gleam at them from the lake's edge, its body hidden under the lap of the gentle waves.

'Hey, we can sleep in this cave tonight,' says Caius, stepping across the rocks. He stretches out his hand and Nona takes it once again and lets him lead her into the musky, damp, cavernous hole.

The inside of the cave is dark, but Nona's eyes quickly get accustomed to it. She sniffs the air and drops down onto all fours. She can smell something she hasn't smelt in a very long time. It transports her back to her life with the dogs, dragging a carcass across the ground with her teeth, growling and chewing at the sinews of meat around the bone. Then she sees the cave is stacked with them. Some on rock shelves, others in piles against the walls. She nudges Caius.

'What is it?' he says.

'Look! Do you know what they are?'

He stares at them closely.

'Bones, aren't they?'

'Yes, but what sort of bones?'

He grabs hold of her and drags her out into the light. He is shaking.

'I don't know. Some sort of animal, I guess, that goes in there to die.'

'But they're all arranged. What sort of animal would do that?' she says.

And at that moment an agonising sound comes from the heart of the forest. It is a mixture of a human cry and a howl and a roar and it echoes through the trees. It sends a cloud of birds into the air and puts shivers down their spines.

'Jay?' says Nona in alarm.

They clutch each other, their ears straining for the sound to start up again.

And then it comes, ringing out through the frosted air.

'What's your name? My name is Jay Bailey.'

His voice echoes around the forest and the lake and the mountains.

Jay Bailey. Jay Bailey. Jay Bailey.

'Is he all right?' asks Caius.

For a while Nona says nothing, then she turns to him and smiles.

'Yes, I think he is. I think he's finally found himself. You see . . .' She pauses. 'You see, he has the heart of a . . .' She stumbles. 'Oh, *I'll tell you about it one day*. Let's go and find him. It's getting dark.'

They turn together and walk towards Jay and the forest. And as they turn, a group of figures silently watch them, gathered on the horizon, silhouetted in the last warming rays of light.

Acknowledgements

I would firstly like to thank my agent, Suzy Jenvey, who has encouraged me and had such faith in me from the very beginning of this literary journey. Also my wonderful editor, Emma Matthewson, without whom this book would never have been and who is a joy to work with. Enormous thanks to Elinor Bagenal, who has read every single piece of my writing, giving me advice and guidance on the way. Without her I would have just stuck with the poetry. Suzy Alexander and Chloe Coggin, my faithful readers, who pointed out the not-so-good bits and suggested alternative ways to improve the story. Jonah Weston, who sent me his film on *Wild Children*, which gave me the idea to write about my girl who was brought up by dogs. Donovan Glyn from Whipsnade Zoo, who showed me the Asian bears and told me lots of things about them so that my bear, Abel Dancer, could really come to life. Joan Wiles, whose great writing workshops gave rise to the first line in the book. Dr Laser, Jason Sapon, for his advice and help on lasers. The writer Jay Griffiths, whose book *Wild* was truly inspirational, and my friend Bin Scaburri, who gave me the book in the first place. All at Hot Key Books who have worked hard to turn my manuscript into a book, and my daughters, Chloe and Phoebe, for not minding when I just carried on writing.

About the Author

Linda Coggin taught horse riding in the West Indies before studying mime in Paris and Czechoslovakia. As part of a small company, she played the fringe theatres and cabaret circuits of Europe. She appeared in Ken Russell's film *Gothic* as the mechanical doll. She worked as an actor for several years and presented *The Home Show* for Thames Television.

Linda writes and performs her own poetry; her collection entitled *Dog Days* has been published. She lives in Wiltshire with her two children and numerous animals. Follow Linda at www.lindacogsblog.blogspot.co.uk.

Thank you for choosing a Hot Key book.

If you want to know more about our authors and what we publish, you can find us online.

You can start at our website

www.hotkeybooks.com

And you can also find us on:

We hope to see you soon!